How (Not) to Kiss a Beast

Elizabeth A. Reeves

DEDICATION

To those that know love isn't easy, but it can be all the sweeter for the sour... and is never one-note... just like a good dessert.

ACKNOWLEDGMENTS

This story could be honestly attributed to my fans—who have supported me in this series and encouraged me to keep them coming.

Chapter One

"Look like you're enjoying yourself," the photographer Jessi had hired said. "Smile, wider... no, now you look like you're baring your teeth."

I had been baring my teeth. I shot Jessi a dirty look. It was all her fault that I was in this bind. My roommate and best friend knew perfectly well that I hated to be in front of a camera.

"It will be fun," she had coaxed me. "Amanda is an incredible photographer and we need some great promotional shots for the truck."

I didn't understand why I had let her talk me into it. Why did the bakery need my picture? Sure, it carried my name, but surely just anyone could pose as me for the customers, right?

"Can you hold your whisk in the air," the photographer asked, "and let some of the batter fall while you watch?"

I sighed to myself, trying not to roll my eyes. I had already been scolded for ruining a picture by rolling my eyes.

"Isn't this fun?" Jessi giggled, safely out of camera range.

I forced myself to smile, imagining myself bludgeoning my very dearest friend with the camera and the photographer together.

"Perfect!" Amanda shouted. "That is the perfect look."

Great. I looked my best when I was contemplating murder.

"I really need to get back to work," I announced, trying to put an end to the whole photo shoot thing.

"Awesome!" Amanda glowed. "I'll get some candid shots while you do your thing."

Whatever made her happy. I had no intention of catering to her. I had real work to do.

Real work consisted of whipping up some meringue for my spicy chocolate mousse, which featured my favorite blend of Mexican chocolate, chipotle, and real cinnamon. Just thinking about it made my mouth water.

I had made the crusts for the pies out of spicy chocolate cookies, crushed and pressed with butter into the pie tins, before making the chocolate mousse and topping it with my very special meringue—which was basically a riff on a Swiss buttercream, which meant it was sweet and silky... and perfect. I'd put just a touch of coconut in the meringue, which made the whole dessert just over-the-top on the decadence scale.

The decadence scale had been invented by Jessi, who figured our customers wanted to know how deep they were getting in, when it came to ordering our desserts. Each tray sported a little tag with a thermometer on it marked anywhere from 'light' to 'deathly indulgent' with appropriate numbers.

Jessi obviously didn't have enough work to do.

My Sinful Chocolate Mousse was ranked a 9.5 on a scale of ten.

"One of these days," I muttered, "I am going to blow that stupid scale out of the water."

Maybe that had been Jessi's plan all along. I couldn't begin to guess what went on in that devious mind of hers.

"That curly hair hides devil horns," I muttered to my meringue, which was coming together beautifully, with specks of real vanilla in it.

Ever since our roommate had abandoned us to marry the man of her dreams Jessi had been at loose ends. Even her budding romance with a D'jinn didn't seem to keep her out of mischief.

Today it was the photo shoot.

Yesterday it had been organizing the bakery in alphabetical order.

Before that she had gotten it into her head to clean out my spice rack and get them into 'order'. I was still having a hard time finding what I needed and I was pretty sure my precious stash of wasabi had gone to the place from which no food returns.

Unless I did something quick, Jessi was going to drive me crazy.

"I love your hair," the photographer said. "It has such... life to it."

I raised a hand self-consciously to my rather frizzy mop of untamable red curls.

"It's such a great color for you," she continued. "Where do you get it done?"

I got that question a lot. Most redheads don't have my shade of true red as their natural hair color.

"Nowhere," I told her. "This is my natural color."

I could tell that she didn't believe me.

Well, that was on her. I was telling the truth, whether she bought it or not.

"How do you stay so slim, working with so much sugar and butter?" she persisted.

What, was she a journalist now?

I shrugged. "Good metabolism," I muttered. I wasn't about to tell her that the Magic I used to enhance my baked goods burned a lot more calories than I could keep up with.

I slid the chocolate mousse tarts into the fridge to set and pulled out some of yesterday's pumpkin pound cake, which I began to cube.

"What are you making now?" the photographer asked.

I glanced at her, my knife poised for a second and she snapped my picture. I hope I didn't look like some crazy murderer.

"Pumpkin chai bread pudding," I told her. "There's chai in the pumpkin pound cake, but I'm also going to put it in the custard."

She licked her lips.

"You know," she said slowly. "I just got a great idea."

I raised an eyebrow at her.

"You should audition for 'Battling Cupcakes'!" she said in a rush, "You would totally win!"

Of course Jessi loved the idea. "It would be great publicity for the bakery and the truck," she gushed. "Oh, Cindy, we totally should do that!"

I glared at her. "We're swamped as it is," I reminded her. "What makes you think we can take on something as huge as this?"

"It will be fun," Jessi coaxed. "We'll just have to find someone new to work at the shop and..."

I watched her make plans with the photographer with a growing sense of dread.

There was no way I was going to get out of this now.

I let them make plans for my life while I went back to business. I had a full day ahead of me and that wasn't going to change anytime soon.

Jessi was right about one thing—we needed a few extra sets of hands around the bakery if we were going to keep ourselves afloat.

I slid the chai pumpkin bread pudding into the oven and turned to my next task—a special order from a loyal customer, Amy, who happened to be a werewolf... and pregnant.

In my rather limited experience werewolves were already creature with appetites nothing short of Magical. Amy herself could out eat an entire high school basketball team and still end up super model skinny—and that was before she'd gotten pregnant.

These days she had to be eating for at least six or seven... werewolves. As far as I could tell she hadn't even gained a pound, though she insisted that she was already showing.

My 'food baby' was bigger than her real baby.

Amy didn't have any of the nausea or discomfort I was familiar with in a pregnant woman—I'd been there for all of my mother's pregnancies, after all. Instead she was even more energetic than usual, her hair was shinier, and she literally glowed. It must have been from all the creative Magic focused on her.

But she did have cravings, monster cravings, and it was up to me to come up with ways of satisfying her hunger.

I'd been brining pork skin in the fridge overnight in a blend of turbinado sugar, chipotle, cinnamon, maple sugar. raw honey, red pepper, paprika, garlic, tamarind, and sea salt. Now I scored the skin with an ultra-sharp knife and put it in the oven to roast.

My spicy sweet pork rinds were a huge hit in the werewolf community. I'd been making them nonstop for weeks. I'd tried adding the sweet and spicy mixture after baking, but it just hadn't had enough of a kick for my picky customers. The dry rub really packed the flavor into the skin in a great way.

It also was a lot of work, which served as a great distraction from the fact that I hadn't heard from my boyfriend in almost a month.

I couldn't shake the feeling that something horrible had happened to him. I called daily, but his cellphone had quit letting me even leave messages—his voice mail was completely full.

Timothy often traveled in remote areas where phone service could be an issue, but he'd never been gone this long.

Some people binge on chocolate when they're worried. I knew this, I saw it almost every day working in a bakery, but I found my escape in something totally different—I binged on baking.

With Tansy married and whisked off to the middle lands to live with her prince, and my baking assistant Sumac back to my mysterious father, whom she had been spying on me for, we had had to make some serious changes at Cindy Eller Cupcakes.

These days customers got what we served. As I created, Jessi would announce over every social media possible what the day's menu was. Some days we didn't even have a chance to utilize our beautiful pink food truck—we just didn't have enough hands.

The real problem was my big secret—my Magic. Not just anyone could come and work with me without my exposing myself as a real, honest-to-goodness witch.

My last assistant had been a cupid, which had created quite a lot of havoc among our customers. I blamed her for the baby boom among my Ordinary clients.

Amy wasn't the only recently pregnant woman I was catering to these days.

The photographer waved to Jessi and bounced off, beaming with a big bakery sack that assumed was her payment.

"It's settled," Jessi said with evident satisfaction, "we're going to tape your audition soon."

I sighed. "Oh, joy."

Chapter Two

I awoke the next morning to a set of identical faces hovering over me and immediately went on the offensive. "What did you two do now?"

My twin sisters, Rainey and Starrie Skye, sighed as if I had wounded them.

I knew better. My littlest sisters had a real gift for mischief. Maybe that's because they were descendants of the Morrigan—the dark fairy from King Arthur's time. Only it was more complicated than that. Ordinaries had really run with that whole story... poor abused Isolde, his real wife, had never raised her voice at him let alone betrayed him.

I dragged my errant morning brain back to my hovering sisters and folded my arms across my chest.

"Mom says we're driving her crazy," Rainey said plaintively, dropping to her feet and sitting down on my bed.

Starrie sighed. "She told us to go get... jobs." She shuddered at the very idea.

I saw where this was going. "No way," I told them. "I know you're sixteen now and I can legally hire you, but there's no way you're coming to work with me at the bakery."

Two sets of moon-silver eyes lit up.

"I didn't think of that!" Rainey breathed, clasping her hands together. "Oh, please, Cindy! I swear we'll be good!"

"Please let us work for you!" Starrie added her voice to the plea.

I fought the urge to hide my head under my pillow. I knew from experience that ignoring them would not make them go away, just get louder.

I scowled at them. "One single trick and you will regret being born!"

They nodded in unison, grins flooding their pixie-ish faces. The hooked pinkies together. "We promise!"

"No Magic in front of Ordinaries!" I shrieked, but it was too late.

They were already gone.

I unlocked the bakery door completely preoccupied with my own thoughts—which were oscillating between the fact that I was going to have the twins on my hands for long periods of time and the idea of making something really bright and light, yet still warming.

I almost tripped over the man sitting on my doorstep.

"Whoops," I said, righting myself. "I'm sorry, I didn't see you there."

The man looked up at me with a mild expression. His eyes were vague in a rather brown and extremely hairy face. His no-color eyes looked straight past me as if he couldn't register my existence. The way he hunched on the stoop made me wonder if he was ill. He wore shabby brown clothes that had seen better days and the tips of his rather grubby fingers peeped out from a scruffy pair of gloves. Even his knuckles were hairy.

He was just another ordinary person down on their luck, perhaps.

But there was a binding of golden light surrounding him, which meant that he'd been touched by Magic at some point. Serious Magic.

Maybe he was a lost or errant gnome? A bitten werewolf, rather than the usual genetic ones I knew, that was stuck halfway into the change? There was something about him that didn't seem quite Ordinary.

"Are you hungry?" I asked, hoping I didn't sound patronizing. "I can bring you something to eat. Or, if you like, you can eat it out here."

Some Magical creatures got really claustrophobic when it came to being indoors. I didn't want to panic my visitor, who really did look famished, if his sunken-in cheeks under all the hair were any indication.

He didn't respond, which meant to me that he wasn't opposed to me feeding him. In moments I had heated up a leftover pumpkin chai bread pudding and some of Tansy's strongest coffee. I slid them onto the doorstep next to him with a bottle of water.

"If you need anything else," I told him, "just call. I'm here... well, pretty much all the time."

He looked up at me with no expression on his face, but I still felt warm inside, like I had done something exceptional instead of something just anyone would do.

"Right, then," I said to myself, turning back to my work. "Light, airy, warm, and... sour? Tart?" I rubbed a hand through my wild hair.

The first thing that spoke to me was limes, which I had plenty of thanks to my mother's Magical garden. I knew I could make a super airy creation with those flavors in a whipped up mixture of egg whites, mascarpone cheese, and egg yolks with just enough sugar to stop the pucker power.

It was exactly what I was in the mood for, so I hoped it would hit the same note with my customers.

I'd half expected my sisters to bail on the whole job thing, but they appeared on the dot of six in the back of the bakery. Each of them was laden down with a huge sack, which they dropped with identical moans.

My curiosity was piqued. "What are those?"

Starrie sighed and rolled her eyes. "Mom sent these over."

Rainey nodded. "They're supplies."

I rubbed my hands together in anticipation. Gifts from an Earth Witch (she was actually classified as a Fairy Godmother, though I was unaware of any Godchildren in her repertoire) were always welcome in my bakery, even if I didn't dare use truly Magical ingredients with my Ordinary customers.

I tore into the first huge sack with enthusiasm, squealing as I took in what had to be nearly fifty pounds of gorgeous dates. I popped one into my mouth—it was sticky, sweet and delicious. I already had a thousand ideas for these little nuggets of perfection.

The second parcel held a huge jug of maple syrup— the real stuff. I'd been begging Mom to name her source for years. Having a jug of this rich goodness was almost as good as knowing how to get it myself.

There was also a wrapped bundle of what had to be twenty full pounds of bacon.

"Oh, my gosh," I said reverently, realizing it was from Uncle Brody's farm. He was an Earth Witch with an amazing knack for farming. His bacon was easily the best apple-smoked artisan bacon in the world—other than the flying pig variety, which I would never be able to use in a bakery that catered to the Ordinary. "I think I've died and gone to Heaven. Whatever did I do to deserve this?"

Rainey sniggered. "You're hugging the bacon."

"You two want to be alone?" Starrie added her giggle to her twin's.

"Just you wait," I warned her, laughing as I realized there were actual tears in my eyes after this landfall. "You will get emotional over what I can do with these babies." My eyes narrowed as I took in the sacks again. "What does Mom want?"

"Ah, her sense returns," Starrie teased.

"She wants dibs on everything you make," Rainey said.

I pursed my lips. That didn't sound like our mother, but I wasn't going to question anything. I wanted these ingredients! I'd just have to worry about what scheme was up my mother's graceful sleeves later.

"We're here to help," Starrie said impatiently, jolting me out of my date induced daydream.

I nibbled on my lower lip as I took the pair of them in. They both wore black baby-doll dresses and white pinafores, bringing out the shocking paleness of their skins and the jet black of their heavy bangs. Their matching butterfly tattoos on their necks gave them that little touch of whimsical Magic. They looked adorable and sinister all at once.

I took a deep breath, praying that I had the nerve to deal with the dangerous duo.

"OK," I said firmly, hoping they would take me seriously, "I need Starrie to start pitting the dates. Starchild, do you know how?"

She nodded and immediately started dragging the bag towards the sink.

I turned towards Rainey. "I'll show you what to do. We're going to candy some bacon."

"Can I watch?" Starrie asked from her station. "I want to learn."

I nodded. "Of course. I'll teach you both anything you want to learn."

I was surprised at the excitement that filled me as I started the girls setting out strips of bacon to be brushed down with maple syrup. It was nice to be working with family, I realized. My sisters actually wanted to learn something from me!

I'd spent so much of my life being the odd one out with my power's secretly bound by my mother. I wasn't used to being the successful one.

I set to showing my sisters how to make little individual sticky toffee puddings—with luscious dates in the base of the cakes and a maple bacon toffee sauce with a touch of my favorite smoky chipotle salt to balance out all of the sweet.

Rainey was more methodical about following my instructions, while Starrie had all the questions as we set to work.

"What would happen if we used coconut cream instead of whipping cream for the toffee sauce?" She asked curiously. " Can you whipped both up the same way? And why do you use volcanic salt? Can we use the pink salt instead?"

I grinned. "Instead of just asking me, why don't you try it out? Remember, only one change at a time so you can keep track of what you like and what you don't. If you tweak everything at once you'll never know what worked and what didn't."

Two pairs of eyes widened as they realized the implication of my offering. The youngest children of a control freak like my mother, I doubted they had ever been offered such an opportunity. The twins bent their heads together over one of my pink mixers to try their hands at experimentation.

As long as they didn't burn the shop down they couldn't do that much damage.

I hoped.

Chapter Three

Jessi came into the shop to open it for our customers and paused for a long moment to survey my sisters, still working out the wrinkles in their first recipe. She pointed a finger at them. "No dogs in the bathroom, got it?"

They tittered.

I smothered my own giggle with a date and bacon bar I had been working on. It was pretty darn good, in my un-humble opinion.

She raised an eyebrow, not fooled by my move in the least. She jerked her head towards the front door. "What's with the furry guy on the doorstep? One of your friends?"

I shrugged. "I have no idea," I admitted. I'd forgotten all about him in my excitement over the new ingredients. "He was there this morning when I arrived. He looked hungry." I glanced towards the twins. "Did you have anything to do with this?"

They had a long history of bringing furry things home. As far as mischief, this was something I could deal with.

Starrie and Rainey exchanged glances and stifled a grin.

"Can we keep him?" Starrie asked, batting her eyelashes at me.

"Please?" Rainey begged.

I raised an eyebrow at Jessi.

Jessi nodded. "I have no problem with him, if he doesn't cause any trouble." She narrowed her eyes at my sisters. "Unlike those two back there. Don't think you are fooling me with those sweet and innocent faces!" She shouted her last sentence towards the kitchen, where my sisters had returned to work.

Starrie and Rainey offered her their most angelic smiles.

"I miss Sumac," Jessi muttered, turning towards the register.

"I miss Tansy," I sighed, adding a scoop of tamarind paste to my bar mixture.

"Yeah." Jessi looked blue for about three seconds total before she snapped out of it. "You have an audition, by the way."

I blinked at her, almost dropping too much candied bacon into my mixture. "What are you talking about? An audition for what?"

She shook her head, her vibrant curls making a soft halo around her face. "Um, duh? The Battling Cupcakes show?"

"Oh, no!" I shook my head at her. "No way! I thought you were just kidding about that whole thing. There's no way I'm going to do something like that!"

Jessi ignored me. "You audition in a week," she said blithely, smiling at our first customer of the morning.

"Are you forgetting something?" I demanded. I dropped my voice to a whisper as the customer perused our display cases. "Like how we're supposed to hide my Magic?"

Jessi shrugged. "We'll figure something out," she said confidently.

"Oh, great," I moaned. "I'm going to be exposed on film as a witch. The whole Ordinary world will find out and start World War Three! I'm going to end up in front of the Council again for sure and it will all be your fault."

"Just think of how great this kind of publicity will be for the bakery," Jessi said cheerfully, handing the customer her box of pastry and waving. "Have a nice day!"

"I can't do it," I told her seriously. "There is no way I can audition for the show."

"We love Battling Cupcakes!" Starrie announced behind us. "Are you really going to be on the show? You're going to be so famous!"

Great. All I needed was my sisters and Jessi to start enabling each other.

"No," I repeated, "no, I won't do it."

As usual, nobody listened to me.

I was rather grumpy by the time I left the bakery in the afternoon to head to my regular lessons with Stephan, my stepfather. There was nothing like being completely walked over to get me panty's bunched up, which Jessi announced was my problem as I was leaving.

"You are forgetting one big thing," I told her for what had to be the fiftieth time. "How am I supposed to hide my Magic when I'm being broadcast on TV? Don't you think that would kind of make it obvious that I'm a witch?"

"We'll take care of that," Starrie said confidently, tossing her dark hair over her shoulder.

"Yeah, we can mask you, no biggie," Rainey added. "There is one really important question, though."

I raised an eyebrow at her. Since when was masking Magic no biggie? "What's that?" I asked her.

"Which one of us are you going to take as your assistant?"

Both girls stared up at me with hopefully expectant eyes.

"Ugh." I made a face. "I'm late for my lesson. I'm out of here. Just don't bring anymore furry creatures here, OK?"

I left them to planning the rest of my life and headed towards the local Tacos y Margaritas, where a secret portal to Magic Central resided in the lady's room.

I really needed my sisters to show me their transportation spell. I was spending way too much time trotting in and out of a bathroom at all hours of the day and night.

I juggled two big boxes of treats in my hands—one for my mom and one for Stephan—as I passed through the portal and made my way through the mayhem that was Magic Central.

Stephan gave me lessons in the werewolf club where he had his own private set of rooms. I often wondered why he had chosen such a location, and figured that it was to get some relief from my mother. She had to be pretty upset to brave both werewolves and the dodgy ghoul doorman that worked there. My mother was a bit of a Magical snob.

I only knew of one time that she had taken refuge there, and she had been hiding from me.

At least the doorman wasn't a zombie. Zombies gave me the creeps big time.

I found Stephan in his customary chair with book in his hands and a cat on his knee.

My cat.

"Merlin," I greeted with a sigh. I was growing accustomed to my unusual cat coming and going as he pleased. It shouldn't surprise me to find him hanging out with my stepfather. "Stephan."

My stepfather closed his book with a smile as I handed him the two boxes I'd brought from the bakery.

"Dates, bacon, and maple syrup are the flavors of the day," I told him. "Tell my mother thank you for the gifts."

A wry smile touched Stephan's lips. He opened the lid of the box I gestured to and the smile widened as he took in the array of tiny tea cakes he preferred to keep in stock.

Werewolves, ghouls, and tea... those were how my stepfather managed to live with a woman like my mother.

Hey, whatever worked for them.

Of my multitude of stepfathers over the years, Stephan was by far my favorite. And it wasn't just because he loved my dessert creations. He never tried to father me, while at the same time he was always available to help me sort out my Magical issues, which were many and varied.

Plus, he really loved my baking.

"I have a project for us," I announced, settling into my chair and patting my lap for Merlin to join me.

My traitorous cat hesitated for one long moment before making the transfer. I shot him a dirty look as he finally decided to pick me. I smoothed his long, soft fur as he took his seat on the arm of my chair, where he could watch everything we did.

Stephan didn't look up from his teapot until both of our cups we filled. He handed me mine and the scent of ginger and peppermint wafted up my nose.

Soothing.

"What project do you have in mind?" my stepfather asked as he sipped his tea and settled a plate of my goodies on his knee.

"I want to try to scry again," I told him. "I know you said it was dangerous for me—with my father and all that—but I need to see if we can find Timothy." I bit my lower lip. "I think something bad must have happened to him."

Stephan frowned in thought. "I should be able to shield you," he said doubtfully. "I trust your instincts. If you think we should do this—that there is a real need for it—we will give it a try."

I turned to Merlin. "Well? What do you think?"

His purr was far more reassuring than Stephan's uncertainty.

I rubbed my hands together. "OK," I said. "Let's do this."

Stephan cleared off the little table so we could set up his large scrying bowl. He filled it with water from the teapot and spoke words over it until the water was perfectly smooth and calm.

Merlin shifted his weight from the arm of the chair onto my lap, like a furry anchor. He circled once and sat where I could lean on him—both Magically and physically. I could feel my powers steady and flow from me through him and then back again. Merlin was more than my cat. Witches of old would have called him my familiar. The two of us were connected Magically.

Stephan dimmed the lights as I concentrated on clearing my mind. I didn't want any distractions like I had had the last time I tried this.

I needed to make sure Timothy was OK.

I focused my mind's eye on Timothy as I had last seen him—handsome, smiling, with his dark blond hair, hazel eyes, and beautiful dimples. My heart squeezed at the memory.

I would do almost anything to see him again.

I opened my eyes and focused my powers on the water.

At first, nothing happened. Then images began to sweep across the surface of the water—a third person view of me and Merlin looking into the bowl while Stephan watched on—a grave covered in roses while a teenaged boy knelt beside it—Tansy laughing with a golden-haired little boy in her arms.

"Timothy," I directed, not letting myself be distracted. "Show me where Timothy is."

The waters went completely dark for a long moment.

I swallowed hard, what could that mean? Did it mean that Timothy was... dead?

The bowl flashed with a sudden, piercing golden light. I jerked back with a shriek, momentarily blinded. I blinked against the after-image behind my eyelids. When my eyes cleared there was a familiar face in front of me— but not the one I was looking for.

"Sumac?" I demanded.

Sue looked straight at me, her dainty brows lifted in surprise. "Cindy?"

Her voice sounded odd—as if it was coming from a long distance and had a hollowness that I guessed was from the water.

Sumac glanced around herself with a decidedly nervous air. "Cindy," she whispered. "We have trouble."

"What kind of trouble?" I demanded.

Sumac made a hushing gesture. "I can't talk to you about it—I'm forbidden. All I can say is... your father doesn't approve of your Ordinary boyfriend and he has taken matters into his own hands."

"What does that even mean?" I could hear my voice rising to a squeak as it had a tendency to do when I was worried. "He didn't—"

Sumac shook her head quickly. "He didn't kill him," she said. "But—Cindy, I really *can't* tell you anything. Just... keep your eyes open, OK?"

Before I could protest, she made a sweeping motion with her hand and the image was gone.

I was back to looking at the reflection of my own face in the water.

"Well," Stephan said, raising the lights, "that was certainly interesting. Your abilities always take me by surprise."

"Me, too," I said dryly. "I suppose it isn't 'normal' to have a conversation through a scrying bowl?"

He chuckled. "Not at all, but we don't really know what effect your heredity will have on your powers. Perhaps this sort of thing is more usual... there."

There. My stepfather was referring, of course, to the fact that I was the product of an illicit (and illegal) relationship between my mother and a man from Faerie. According to my mother and Sumac he was something between an angel and what most Ordinaries would have associated with the Greek gods.

As Faerie and our world were banned from having contact, no one knew what that could mean for me.

And I'd only known for a few weeks.

"Timothy's in trouble," I said, rubbing my eyes. They still stung from that flash of light. "That much was clear."

Stephan nodded soberly, rubbing his upper lip in thought. "At least you know he's alive."

"Yes, at least there's that."

Chapter Four

I was relieved to find my little bakery still intact when I returned. I had half expected to find it either missing entirely or reduced to rubble, with my sisters and Jessi in charge.

Instead, I found the whole shop neat, orderly, and my sisters cheerfully following a recipe I had written out for them.

My eyes narrowed. They had to be up to something. They were *always* up to something.

Jessi was going through a stack of papers next to the register. She, at least, had relaxed enough to let her guard down with those two around.

Ah, the naiveté.

"What are these?" I asked, picking up a sheet and seeing what looked like a resume.

"We're interviewing bakers," Jessi announced, "and looking for a new roommate."

I made a face. I'd been avoiding admitting the fact that Tansy wasn't going to be coming back to live with us. She was happily married now—and living far, far, away—in the true fairy tale sense. There was no real reason her rooms should stay empty, but if felt almost sacrilegious to think of someone else living there.

"I still think you should move into Tansy's suite," Jessi was saying. "It has its own bathroom and the bigger bedroom."

Tansy had slept in the master bedroom of the house we'd rented together for over a year, while Jessi and I slept in the smaller bedrooms and shared a bathroom.

I shrugged. "The space would be nice... but, it feels weird, you know? I would feel like I was in Tansy's space, not my own."

Jessi shrugged.

"This whole thing," I said. "Do we really need another roommate? I mean—what if they found out about my Magic?"

"Taken care of," Jessi said smugly. "Alecto helped me post the ads where only Magic folk would see them."

I fought the urge to sigh. Jessi's boyfriend was a D'jinn and I trusted him about as much as I would a PMS-ing werewolf to guard a banquet. Which meant: not at all.

I never wanted to be racist in the Magical world, but D'jinn didn't have the cleanest reputation–they were generally known as untrustworthy and sly—and that was the best of them. There were other stories, too—the kind that could make skin crawl and blood attempt to freeze. Not pretty.

I just didn't want to see my best friend get hurt.

Jessi didn't want to hear anything bad about him, though. If I even suggested that she be careful she would give me a 'drop dead' look and suggest that I mind my own business. She thought she could handle anything he might throw at her.

I just hoped she was right.

She was playing with fire—literally if the D'jinn creation story of being made of eternally burning fire was true. She might think she could handle anything, but I didn't want her to get burnt.

After all, she was my best friend.

"That was nice of him," I said, trying to keep my feelings about Alecto out of my voice. It wasn't my place to tell her who she could date. "Any good prospects so far?"

Jessi shrugged one shoulder. "I don't know," she admitted. "I can't tell. There are werewolves..."

"Noisy once a month and eat a lot," I interjected.

"Sounds like most women," she nodded. "And then there's an application from an imp?"

I peered at the sheet she gave me. "Bad idea," I told her. "I don't know why an imp would want to live with Ordinaries, but it's never a good reason. They feed off of chaos. Literally."

Jessi sighed. "See? Why can't we just find a nice witch..."

"Mom doesn't let us use that word," Rainey said from behind me.

"She says that it creates prejudice," Starrie added.

"She's so full of it," they chorused together.

Starrie grabbed a sheet of paper and read it over. "Why don't you see if Iris wants to live with you?" she suggested. "She's between apartments at the moment."

I hadn't known that. Iris was my second sister and nearly four years younger than me. She was a bit of a free spirit, which drove my mother crazy, but I tried to encourage partly *because* it made my mother crazy.

"That would be awesome," Jessi said, practically glowing and clapping her hands enthusiastically. "Iris is fun!"

I nodded. If I had to have a new roommate, it might as well be my sister.

It was better than a complete stranger.

Iris was over-the-top excited about the idea of living with me and Jessi. She tended to get that way sometimes. I always put it down to an artistic temperament.

"What's going on?" I asked her over the phone once she had finished gushing about how amazing it was going to be to live together and how she was going to be the best roommate ever. "Why are you even looking for a place to live? I thought you were pretty settled!"

Iris sighed. "I just can't do it," she said dramatically. "I want to make Mom happy and everything, but I'm a dissertation shy of a doctorate in Architecture and all I want to do is find a way to express myself artistically in any other medium than blueprints and buildings." She paused. "Speaking of which. Do you need any more help in the shop?"

I laughed. "You want to work for me, too? Wow. If we keep this up we're going to be running a family business over here. Do you really need a job?"

"Absolutely." Iris answered. "I can start immediately, too. I can't wait to get out of all this banality and really start tapping into my true creativity again."

I'd almost forgotten how much I adored Iris. I was already grinning from ear to ear talking to her.

Maybe Jessi was right. Maybe we needed something like this to move on.

"Deal," I said. "You can move into Tansy's suites right away."

"Ha!" she laughed. "I should have guessed you would get all big-sister on me and try to give me the best rooms in the house. No way. No how. I'll take your rooms and *you* can move into Tansy's room. Oh, and I'm bringing Chloe and my parrot, OK?"

"Of course." Chloe was Iris's pet bat and practically the smallest bat in the universe. You could hold her on one fingernail, she was so tiny.

She was pretty adorable.

"I'll just tell Merlin that she's off limits," I told Iris. "I make no promises about the parrot."

"Ha!" Iris laughed. "As if that fat cat could even catch her!"

"He's not fat," I protested.

"He eats way too many pastries," Iris answered. "His belly is going to start dragging on the floor soon."

"Brat," I told her.

"Bossy," she answered easily. "I'll see you tonight, then. I'll be moved in before you get home."

I opened my mouth to protest, knowing that it would do no good—I'd end up in the suite whether I liked it or not—but she had already hung up on me.

"Life is going to be a whirlwind," I told Jessi, shaking my head. "A rainbow-colored whirlwind at that. Not only is Iris going to come and live with us, but she's also going to work here. Looks like we'll have enough crew to dust off the dessert truck and start making rounds again."

Jessi clapped her hands. "Perfect!" she said. "You should take her to Battling Cupcakes when you go—that should keep your little sisters from squabbling over which one of them gets to go with you."

I sighed. I had almost forgotten about that.

"I've got cupcakes to make," I grouched, making a face at her.

"Good idea," Jessi said cheerfully. "You're less grumpy while you're cooking."

I made a face at her, but went right to work.

Chapter Five

I walked into the door at home and immediately turned around to walk outside. I had to make sure I had the same place. Maybe I had accidentally walked into the wrong house. Sure, from the outside it was still identical to the place I had left this morning, but nothing inside looked the same at all.

Iris sure had moved in quickly.

Gone was my big, comfy, rather lumpy tan couch— the one that practically ate unsuspecting visitors. Gone were my white walls and simple decorations.

The rainbow had struck.

I poked my new scarlet couch with one finger and delightfully realized that she had just re-covered my ultra-comfy one. It sported a mish-mash of orange, brown, and yellow pillows that were new to me, but looked cozy and cute.

Knowing Iris, they were probably handmade.

My living room now had a bright brilliant southwestern orange accent wall with real living ivy climbing all over it. Banana trees sprouted from pots in every corner of the room. Some branches actually appeared to be growing straight out of the wall. A live parrot sat on a brass perch to one side, happily grooming itself, all part of the tropical air that Iris had created in there.

After all, my sister was an Earth Witch.

Jessi entered on my heels and looked around, whistling under her breath. "Nice," she murmured. "It's like a whole new house."

I nodded, sniffing the air. It smelled like sandalwood, one of my favorite scents. It accented the new, exotic flavor of the house.

The makeover hadn't been reserved to the living room, either. There were new book cases lining the family/dining room and the kitchen had new cabinet doors—the kind where you could see really cute china and dishes through the little windows.

The dishes were new too. Mine were not cute enough to want to look at through glass panels.

She'd somehow even found the time to install a new tile backsplash with touches of cobalt blue and dove gray.

"I wonder if she redid my room," Jessi pondered, turning around and around to capture the full effect of all the changes. "If she didn't, I'm going to ask her if she will. She's got a serious eye for color."

I'd have to take Jessi's word on that. I was artistically rather hopeless.

Speaking of artists, where was my sister?

I traced the brilliant colors down the hallway and back towards my room—my old room, I assumed–where I found my sister blissfully painting away in a pair of old overalls and a man's wife-beater, with her rainbow hair pulled back in a ponytail. Chloe, her miniature bat, decorated her hair-tie like a little dark gem.

Iris bounced around when she heard us and waved. "Isn't this wonderful?" she demanded dramatically, throwing out her arms to embrace the whole world. "It's freedom after all that schooling, I tell you! No more lectures! No more classrooms! I can't wait to get to work tomorrow and really throw myself into creativity again."

"Looks like you already have," I teased, taking in the mural she was working on.

A gorgeous jungle scene sang out at me with a million colors from her wall. I could practically hear the roar of the waterfall and the calls of the wild birds in the distance. A huge silky black panther slept in a ray of dappled sunshine in the foreground, so real that I almost felt like I could reach out and touch the velvet of his coat. His half-lidded eyes sparkled like jewels.

I didn't know how she did it.

"This?" She waved her brush, getting blue paint on her cheek and not seeming to mind. "This is nothing at all. Just you wait—there will be masterpieces! There will be... color! Light! Beauty!"

A couple birds peeled off of the wall behind her and flapped away into the room, startled by her enthusiasm.

I laughed, shaking my head at her. "She gets this way sometimes," I told Jessi, who was regarding this flow of creativity with utter astonishment written all over her face. "Just you wait—she goes the other direction sometimes too."

"It's all creativity!" Iris exclaimed. "Up! Down! Up! Down! It's quite a ride! Life's too short to be boring all the time."

I smiled wryly. "I'll take your word on that. Now... where exactly is my stuff?"

She waved her brush absently towards the hallway and Tansy's suite. I noticed that the paint was now green. At the gesture another painted bird hopped out of the painting and flew around the room.

I hoped my sister never painted in public.

"I set your room up to thank you for putting up with me," she said comfortably, tugging at the bib of her overalls and frowning at her wall. She dabbed a bit of paint in one corner, creating a mountain in just a couple tiny brush strokes. In her hair, I could just barely see Chloe raise her head to eye the results and squeak in what I assumed had to be approval.

My sister totally blew my mind when she did stuff like that.

Sure, I could take different flavors and marry them together to create a kind of masterpiece, but I wasn't a true artist—not like Iris.

I wondered what it would be like to be able to paint like that—to create something so real and vibrant from nothing more than an image in my head.

I decided to check out what Iris had done to Tansy's suites for me. After what she had done to the rest of the house, I had no idea what to expect.

I shouldn't have worried that I would feel like I was intruding into Tansy's territory at all. It didn't even look remotely the same. Instead of pink, the walls were now my favorite shade of blue on three walls, with the fourth wall a complimentary shade of green, all with flowering vines climbing all everywhere. Citrus trees and star jasmine lined the walls of the room, their blossoms filling the air with a sweet perfume.

I closed my eyes and inhaled deeply.

It was paradise.

Iris had carried the redecorating into the bathroom, where the luxurious garden tub was surrounded by more greenery and more flowers. Gardenias drooped seductively in one corner, filling the air with their heady scent.

I really hoped Iris was going to maintain all these plants. I had a bit of a black thumb, to my mother's eternal dismay. I hated to think what would happen to all of this beauty with me in charge. It could go from lush paradise to Sahara in days.

"Don't worry," Iris said, when I asked her. She adjusted her potted irises on the kitchen counter until they were all perfectly in line, "I know you well enough to have thought of that already. They have mom's best spells on them for longevity and I will make sure they stay watered and stuff... just, don't touch them, OK?"

I laughed. I could live with that bargain. "Deal."

She dug into the freezer and pulled out a pint of ice cream. It was one of the flavors Timothy and I had come up with together—the perfect blending of mango and real vanilla.

I missed Timothy so much.

I rubbed my head.

I felt a flash of rage towards the father I had never met. How dare he step in and interfere with my life? He couldn't dictate who I could and couldn't date. He knew nothing about me or Timothy and he had just randomly decided that we didn't belong together?

I'd just have to find a way to get Timothy out of his clutches and be reunited with my former toad.

"How does Mom feel about this career change of yours?" I asked, watching Iris devour her entire pint of ice cream in moments flat. She really did do everything with vive and vigor. "I assume you've told her already?"

"Nope," Iris declared, licking her spoon clean and putting her finished pint in the garbage in one graceful motion. "What she doesn't know can't hurt me."

I snorted. "She's going to be super pissed off when she finds out."

Iris shrugged. "It's my life, right? I have to learn how to be happy without trying to make Mom proud. After all, that's what she has you for."

"Me?" I gaped at her. "I'm the disappointment of her life!"

Iris sniggered. "To your face, perhaps. The rest of us get to hear how wonderful and accomplished you are, owning your own business at such a young age and all that."

I shook my head in disbelief. "That woman!" I marveled.

"Yup," Iris agreed. She peeked into the fridge and made a face as she realized that it was empty. "Don't you guys ever eat anything except ice cream? Do you need me to handle the grocery shopping? You know I'm a mean hand with that couponing stuff."

I nodded. I was pretty sure she cheated at the whole 'extreme couponing' game—with Magic. I wasn't going to complain if I was the one who was going to reap the benefits of it. "Sure. Just get whatever you want. Jessi and I aren't picky at all."

Iris rolled her eyes. "And yet you use nothing but the best ingredients at the bakery."

I grinned. "Of course. That's when it really matters, right?"

She grabbed her purse and coupon folder off of the counter. "I'm going to go shopping," she announced. "I'll be back in, oh, four hours or so. Don't wait up."

"Be at the bakery at eight tomorrow," I called after her. "We have a full day ahead of us."

"No problem, Boss!" she called over her shoulder.

I shook my head with a laugh.

Things were sure going to be different with Iris around.

Chapter Six

Working alongside three of my sisters at once was far easier than I would have ever expected. So far the twins had kept their noses clean and not made too much trouble—though I had caught them 'accidentally' swapping my chipotle for cayenne just in the nick of time.

I was still waiting for them to do something truly mischievous, but so far they had kept their noses pretty clean.

Iris was in happy land, creating, painting, covering cakelets and cupcakes with the most creative decorations I had ever seen in pastry. Her lifelike rose petals on top of my strawberry-rose cupcakes with rose-water scented cream made me almost reconsider that whole Battling Cupcakes thing—with me on flavors and her on decorating, maybe we would actually have a chance at winning.

It was almost enough to make me lose my hatred of competition.

Almost, but not quite.

I handed a croissant and a cup of coffee to the furry guy, who was still sitting outside of my shop. I had invited him in many times, but he didn't seem interested. He looked down at the croissant with his expressionless face and then back up at me.

What was it about those eyes that seemed so... intriguing? Strange?

According to the twins they had found him wandering around and decided he would make a great mascot for the bakery.

I shrugged it off, handing him a bottle of water. "If you need anything," I told him, "Just let us know... somehow. If you want to wash up in the restroom or anything..." I shrugged. "Just, if you need anything at all..."

I wasn't sure he could even understand me. He just looked past me like he always did.

At least he started nibbling on the croissant as I went back into the shop.

"Tomorrow," Iris announced, "we're going to all wake up with Cindy and do morning yoga together. It will help prepare us for the day and get us working together in unity."

I stared at her. Yoga? In the morning? At *four* in the morning?

Was she absolutely out of her mind?

"It will be fun!" she said enthusiastically, ignoring the many sets of eyes that were staring at her as if she were bonkers. "You'll feel muscles you've never even used before."

"At least Tansy never asked us to do yoga at four in the morning," I muttered to Jessi as I walked by her.

"She's your sister," she muttered back.

Just to be contrary, the twins apparently thought morning yoga was a fantastic idea.

"It will be so cool!" Starrie enthused. "Did you know that Iris can put both of her legs behind her head... without the help of Magic?"

"Can you cheat at yoga with Magic?" Jessi asked hopefully.

I shook my head. "Not that I'm aware of," I said ruefully. "We're just going to have to stick it out."

Yoga was even harder than I had imagined. I wasn't flexible in the least and my toes didn't want to have anything to do with my hands. Downward facing dog was sheer agony. The only pose I liked at all was the one where I got to curl up in a fetal ball and doze off.

Sticking it out was an apt phrase—by the time we had twisted, bent, and stretched through an hour that should have been spent sleeping, I was sticky with sweat. I was also pretty sure I stank like a submarine sailor.

"Isn't it so soothing?" Iris glowed as I dragged my aching bones back to my room for a shower. I passed the garden bathtub sadly, wishing I had time for a long soak—my muscles were already starting to tighten up.

"Soothing is not what I would call it," I muttered to myself as I doused myself with pumpkin-pie body wash. Iris's pet parrot had enjoyed my agony a little too much, with his quips of encouragement. "Relax into it! Relax into it!"

Really? I could barely touch my toes. How was I supposed to relax into a downward facing dog?

Well, Iris was right about one thing—I was using muscles I didn't even know I had—and every single one of them was screaming in protest.

"I hate yoga," I told Merlin as I brushed through my thick red hair and attempted to tame it into a knot on the back of my head.

He looked up from his relaxed and impossible feline position and I sighed. Cats just couldn't understand yoga troubles. They were all just too darn flexible.

"I should have gotten a dog," I muttered.

Merlin flicked his ears back, offended.

I soothed his fur back. "I'm sorry," I told him. "I don't want a dog. I want you. I'm just extremely sore and grumpy. Do you forgive me?"

Merlin ignored me as he went back to licking his paw and rubbing it all over his face.

I hoped that meant he'd forgiven me. I hated to think what it would mean if my familiar was unhappy with me the next time I tried to work some serious Magic.

Iris decided to come into the bakery with me, early, instead of waiting to come in at the usual time that Jessi and the twins did. She bounced through the shop with all of her sickening energy.

"Did you even get any sleep last night?" I demanded, as I took my yoga frustrations out on dough that had been in the fridge overnight. It was stiff enough that it could really use the beating I was giving it, if it ever wanted to grow up to be cinnamon rolls.

I was still on my bacon and dates kick. I already had plans to make my filling out of date paste, cinnamon, chipotle, maple syrup, and salty cubed bacon chunks. It was going to be insanely delicious.

Iris hummed to herself as she decorated bon bons, using edible glitter and paints, gumpaste and fondant as her artistic mediums. I thought my treats always looked wonderful, but I had to admit she was taking them to the next level. These treats wouldn't have looked out of place at a five-star restaurant.

Not bad for a tiny little storefront and food truck in Arizona.

"Jessi's right," I said, surveying her tray as she loaded it into the display case, "I should totally take you as my assistant to Battling Cupcakes."

Iris's eyes widened. "Really?" she squealed, clasping her hands together in glee. "You would do that? That would be... incredible!"

I shrugged. "If I have to go, I might as well do my best to kick butt—and that means taking you along. With your decorations I don't see how we could lose."

Iris threw her arms around me and squeezed me so tightly I actually couldn't breathe for a moment. I gently pried her away from me. "We don't even know if we'll get on the show yet," I reminded her.

She grinned confidently under her thatch of rainbow streaks. "We will. I just know it."

Jessi came in at her usual time to open the shop to the public only moments after the twins literally appeared in the back of the bakery, ready and willing to work.

With Rainey and Starrie helping me bake and Iris taking over the decorations, we actually had enough treats to send Jessi and Iris off with the dessert truck to make some rounds.

"Our fans are ecstatic," Jessi announced as they left, waving her phone at me, where she had been hitting the social media big time. "I've given everyone a heads-up and I've already gotten a huge response. I bet we'll be back in no time to restock."

I grinned. It felt like things we finally getting back to some kind of normal, even with Tansy gone. Part of me hated it, but I knew I couldn't let my business suffer because I missed my friend.

Plus, she was disgustingly happy where she was.

"I'll take the register," Starrie announced, once the other two were gone. "Rainey will help you keep baking." She started straightening out the cases and polishing the counter with a rag with the air of a much older professional.

If only I didn't always have that niggling feeling at the back of my mind that she was scheming away behind that angelic facade.

"We want to keep our jobs," Rainey said, as if reading my thoughts. "We're not going to do anything to sabotage that."

"You're keeping up with your schoolwork?" I asked. The girls did schoolwork through an online witch academy, supposedly. I had yet to see them do so much as pick up a book.

"Easy," Starrie intoned in a bored voice.

"We'll be graduated by summer," Rainey added, equally bland.

I shook my head at them. It was almost a family tradition to graduate from high school and college early.

At least Mom wouldn't be on my case about them.

I didn't have much hope that the same would be true when she found out about Iris quitting her Architecture program to work at the bakery with me.

It just wasn't going to be pretty.

Chapter Seven

I was trying my hand at making a maple cream pie—just having added the whipped cream to the maple syrup caramel custard base—when my phone rang. I tucked it under my ear to answer it.

"Cindy?" It was my sister, Rose. I frowned to myself. I hadn't heard from her at all since she had left on her honeymoon, and considered that to be a good sign.

"Hi, Rose," I answered. "I hope everything is OK with you and the new husband?"

"Oh, gosh, yes," her voice practically glowed through the receiver. "We're so happy—oh, Cindy! Thank you for working everything out for us! I couldn't be happier!"

Which is why I was absolutely shocked to hear her then whisper. "Hold on a second." Followed by the most un-happy retching sounds imaginable.

I had a hunch what that was about. After all I was the oldest of six girls—or had been until my mother adopted Tansy. Now I was the second of seven.

"Rose," I said, when she had returned. "Are you... pregnant?"

She giggled, sighed, and giggled again. "Yes. I'm pregnant. I can hardly believe it myself, but I just got a confirmed positive on one of those pee-stick thingies. It's kind of funny, though, because I've been feeling sick for almost a week. I guess my body knew right away, even if the tests didn't."

I really didn't know how to feel about Rose being pregnant. It had taken me a while—longer than it should have, really—to become accustomed to the idea that my little sister had gotten married before I had. Now she was going to have a baby?

I wasn't quite jealous—after all I had heard her just puke her guts out, but I wasn't sure that I was precisely happy for her, either.

Well, I was happy for her, just less happy than I should have been.

"You wouldn't believe it," she was cooing, back to her sickly-sweet in love self, "but the cravings have already hit me full force. If I'm not barfing I'm stuffing my face. You've got to help me! I'm craving all kinds of crazy stuff... like dates. Do you remember how much I hated dates when we were little?"

Yes, I did. And I happened to have an abundance of dates at the moment.

Coincidence? Or had my mother scented something on the wind? You could never be sure.

"I happen to have a lot of dates at the moment," I said dryly. "Any other cravings?"

"Um, well," she giggled. "You know that stinky stuff? That horrible fruit?"

I frowned as I considered it. "Wait, you're not craving durian are you?!"

"Oh, my gosh, no," she said with a titter. "I just wanted to hear your voice when you believed that I was craving it."

I laughed. "You are positively evil."

"Something like that," she agreed. "You wouldn't happen to have... pork rinds, do you?"

I laughed. "Oh, Rose, you have no idea. I am the pregnant woman's delight these days. I'll hook you up."

"Oh good," the relief was palpable in her voice. "Now I just have to get some of that tea Mom used to make when she had morning sickness. You remember it, right?"

"Who could forget?" I answered. "Ginger and peppermint." I paused, frowning to myself. Where had I seen that combination recently? I shrugged. It probably wasn't important. I'd been around so many pregnant ladies lately that it probably had been from one of them.

"How can I ever thank you?" my sister gushed through the phone. "If there's anything I can do..."

"If I think of anything I'll let you know," I promised. "Meanwhile, you could distract Mom for me... She's going to flip out."

"Why?" Rose asked.

"Iris is living and working with me," I told her. "She dropped out of her architecture program."

"Yikes," Rose said sympathetically. "I don't envy you when Mom finds out. Well, I'll try to distract her, but you know that only works for so long with her."

"Unfortunately," I said glumly.

"Hey, Boss," Jessi said, as she came into the shop to restock the dessert truck.

I raised my eyebrow at her. "What do you want?"

She grinned. "You know me so well. Actually, it's more for Alecto."

"Oh," I grimaced at her mention of her D'jinn boyfriend.

"Don't be too quick to say no," Jessi said in a rush. "I was thinking that we could really use help in the truck—you know, taking orders and driving and stuff. Alecto's pretty hot, even you have to admit that. I bet it would be great for attracting business. Sexy guy, pork rinds, we can't miss with that combination."

"True," I admitted. "Well, I guess we can give it a try, if you think he'll keep his nose clean and... I'm sure I don't have to tell you: absolutely no Magic."

Jessi nodded. "No Magic? No problem!"

I nibbled on my lower lip. I didn't have any real reason to mistrust Jessi's boyfriend, but I was filled with misgiving. It was one thing to stay out of their relationship, but quite another to hire him into my fledgling business.

What was that saying about keeping enemies closer? I didn't consider Alecto an enemy, but there was something about him that just didn't sit right with me.

Well, it looked like I was going to have him under my nose from now on anyway.

"Everyone loves the date bars," Jessi mentioned, surveying an Iris-decorated bon bon with an appreciative grin, "even if they're only a 5.5 on the decadence scale. They're going strong with the Paleo crowd. Have you thought about doing more variations on those?"

I pursed my lips. "I'll have to do that," I agreed. "They're pretty versatile."

The bell over the door rang and we both turned to greet our new customer.

My breath caught in my chest. I had to reach out and grab the counter to steady myself.

It was Timothy.

Chapter Eight

"Timothy!" I gasped. "Wh–you're here! Where have you been? Oh, my gosh–I've missed you so much!" I circled around the counter and put my arms around him.

He seemed so stiff and strange as he returned the hug, but I didn't care.

"You're here," I sniffed, fighting hard not to blubber all the way down his shirt front. "I missed you so much! I've been so worried!"

"Cindy," he said, smiling down at me with those amazing dimples of his. "Why would you be so silly? Of course I've been fine."

I frowned. "Fine? I've been calling you every day for weeks!"

"Oh, that," he shrugged. "My phone died."

I could feel my eyebrows draw together in confusion.

"Why don't you two take off for a little while?" Jessi suggested, coming to my rescue. "I'm sure you have lots of catching up to do. It's been so long."

I smiled my thanks as Timothy took my arm and guided me out of the shop.

A flash of fur hurdled into Timothy, knocking him away from me.

"Stop!" I shrieked, throwing myself after my hairy friend from the doorstep. "Don't hurt him!" I wasn't sure who I was talking to—I didn't want either of them injured.

Hairy Guy stopped in mid grapple and backed away from Timothy, his eyes on my face.

"Don't hurt him," I repeated, trying to make my voice soothing. Maybe the twins were right—he certainly was acting like a watchdog for the bakery at the moment.

He seemed to understand me. He backed the rest of the way from Timothy and went back to crouching by the wall near the door of the bakery.

"I don't know what came over him," I explained, as I took Timothy's arm again. "He's really very sweet and gentle. I know he's harmless."

"He probably thought I was hurting you," Timothy suggested, his dimples popping into view again. "He'll just have to learn that I'm here to stay."

I smiled shyly up at him. After all this time it almost felt like starting over. "Are you?" I asked quietly.

"Of course," he answered, as if shocked that I had even questioned him. "Now that I'm home I'm never going to leave you alone again."

Why did that feel so... strange?

I sighed at myself. What was wrong with me? I had exactly the thing I wanted the most—Timothy back with me.

Maybe it just was that I hadn't seen my boyfriend in over a month and now it just felt unreal that he was here, standing in front of me, holding my hand.

I just needed to get used to seeing him again. Maybe I had gotten used to being on my own. I needed to just give him a chance and the weirdness would pass.

Wouldn't it?

"You look great," I told Timothy as we sat down at the little Greek cafe right down the street from my bakery. It was one of my favorite places for a quick bite to eat.

Timothy really did look great—he looked healthy and even his skin had an almost ethereal luster too it. Wherever he had been he had gotten a lot of sunshine to get a tan like that.

He was dressed up—for him—in a button-up shirt and trousers. He looked handsome and well put together.

I felt a little self-conscious in my typical work outfit—a dark t-shirt over my 'artistic' jeans and a kerchief over my abundance of crazy hair, which was desperately trying to escape from the knot at the back of my head. At least I was no longer wearing my apron, though there was still flour all over my jeans.

Next to Timothy, I looked positively Bohemian.

I really needed to start paying attention to how my mother did her stay-neat spells. I wasn't used to my Magic working properly. I kept forgetting that I had real power. I'd probably be able to actually do some of those basic spells now.

Timothy smiled, reaching across the table to take my hand. His fingers felt dry, calm and quiet.

I took a sip of my water to reclaim my fingers and looked down at my gyro. Why hadn't I ordered something that I could eat neatly? The flat bread was practically dripping with grease, an over-abundance of vegetables, and tzatziki sauce. There was no way to dive into it without making a complete pig of myself.

I was hungry, but I didn't want to make a bigger mess.

"So," I said, picking at my gyro and snagging a piece of feta from my plate. "Tell me all about your trip. When did you get home?" I didn't voice the 'where the hell have you been?' that was screaming in the back of my head along with the 'do you have any idea how worried I was?' I couldn't voice any of those without feeling like a complete and utter lunatic.

Timothy shrugged. "It was fine," he said in a blasé voice. "Just another business trip. I'll be glad never to have to do that again."

I wrinkled my nose. What was he talking about?

Timothy had traveled the world since he was sixteen years old—after his mother died and his great-aunt and uncle became his guardians. He loved traveling and finding new flavors to turn into his brand of incredible specialty ice cream. It was one of the things I loved about him—he was so passionate about the way he lived his life.

"You're not going to be traveling anymore?" I asked, biting down on a cherry tomato. The seeds burst out of it and shot across the table.

Timothy dodged it without a thought. "I'm so tired of always being on the road," he said. "I think it's time that I settle down... that we settle down."

I gulped, my mouth suddenly very dry. I choked on the rest of my tomato and had to gulp water to get it down. "Y-you do?" I croaked.

He nodded. "The whole time I was away all I could think about was getting back to you and starting a family.

No more traveling, no more long hours at the bakery for you... we can start our real happily ever after."

I gaped at him. "But," I protested, "I love my job at the bakery!"

He waved his hand dismissively. "You don't need to work, my darling. I will provide for you and you can concentrate on raising our children."

"Children?" I squeaked. "Timothy–"

Again, he waved me to silence. "It will be like a fairytale," he said, blissfully unaware of my sudden urge to strangle him.

I grabbed my water glass and guzzled the whole thing down to hide my frustration and rage. How dare he waltz in here after a month and start planning my life for me? It didn't make sense at all–especially since the last conversation we'd had together had been all about how he wasn't ready to get tied down yet!

I didn't want to argue with him when I'd only had him back for less than an hour.

I needed to change the subject–and fast.

"How are your aunt and uncle?" I asked. "The last I heard they were on a cruise in the Caribbean. That must be a sight for sore eyes! I can't imagine Connie in a bikini!"

I had unwittingly been working for Timothy's great-aunt and uncle, the Davies, when we'd first met.

He frowned at me. "I don't really talk to them much," he said.

I raised an eyebrow at him. That was it? That's all he had to say about the couple that had raised him after his mother's death?

I grimaced as I realized I had another, truly important subject to address with him.

A couple weeks ago a woman had waltzed into my bakery and announced that she was Timothy's mother, Quinna Borden.

Not only was Timothy's mother dead, and had been for years, but this woman had to be about my age, if not a little younger!

"Timothy," I started.

"Hush," he said, brushing tzatziki sauce off of my cheek with his thumb and gazing into my eyes. "We have time to talk about all those inconsequential things for the rest of our lives. Cindy..."

I raised an eyebrow enquiringly.

He smiled down at me tenderly. "Let's run away together," he suggested.

Chapter Nine

"What?" I gasped, yanking my hand away from Timothy's and nearly falling backwards in my chair in the process. "Are you... serious?"

He smiled at me tenderly. "Of course I am serious," he said, brushing back one of my curls with his fingers. "I cannot bear the thought of being without you ever again. Let's run away and get married... tonight."

I frowned. "How about we don't?" I suggested, as gently as I could manage. "I'm flattered, and flabbergasted to be honest, by the change in your opinion about marriage, but you just got home! Can't we just take a little time and get to know each other again?"

He shook his head at me. "Cindy, Cindy, Cindy," he said gently, running his fingers across my cheek as one would caress a cat. "Why must you be so cruel? Always pushing me away like this—how many years must I wait for you?"

I narrowed my eyes at him. "Years?" I asked.

He sighed lovingly. "We should have been married long ago," he informed me, his tone almost chiding. "I have been so patient, letting you get your need to own a business out of your system. We both know that it was nothing more than a game, wasn't it, my dear?"

I jerked away from him and leapt out of my chair–poised between fleeing and tossing the rest of my uneaten lunch at his head.

"What are you talking about?" I demanded. "Timothy–why are you acting so strangely?"

He looked confused. "How do you mean?" he asked, as if I were the one who were acting crazy.

I sucked in a deep breath, trying to calm myself. All of this felt strange–felt wrong. It wasn't supposed to be like this. His homecoming should have been joyous and happy! I should have been ecstatic that he wanted to be with me, but instead I had to fight the urge to run screaming from him.

"Timothy," I said, in a strangled voice. "Did I tell you I saw your mother in the bakery the other day?"

He raised his eyebrows. "Did you?" he inquired. "How's dear old mom doing these days?"

I faked a smile to hide my discomfiture.

I could no longer ignore it. There was something seriously wrong with Timothy.

This wasn't the man I had fallen in love with. This was a stranger–a man who didn't even remember that his mother was dead, a man who seemed to have forgotten every aspect of his life that made him... Timothy.

What had my father done?

I reached out to take his hand, hoping mine wasn't shaking too noticeably.

"Why don't we go get some ice cream?" I suggested.

"Ice cream?" he echoed.

I nodded. "Sure. We'll get your favorite flavor... what was it again?"

His face cleared. "Vanilla," he said confidently.

It took all my effort not to yank my hand away from him.

"So," I said, conversationally, once we were in the car again. "Who are you really, and what did my father promise you to pretend to be Timothy?"

A war of emotions crossed Timothy's familiar yet not familiar face. I could see him waiver between options—confessing the truth or keeping up the pretense.

"You're not him, so don't even try to tell me otherwise," I said, crossing my arms over my chest.

He looked at me for a long moment.

"Who are you?" I demanded. "Let's start with that. And, can you take my boyfriend's face off first, please? You're totally weirding me out."

Even though I had caught on and knew it wasn't really Timothy sitting beside me in the car, I still gasped when his figure swam in front of me and cleared into a quite different form.

I didn't know what I was expecting, but it must not have been anything like reality, for I couldn't help but stare.

For one thing, he was beautiful. I mean, he was masculine in every way, but at the same time... he was way prettier than me.

No way was he human, either.

He had huge, slanted green eyes and a smooth olive complexion. He had masses of short dark curls and the face of a poet.

Or an angel.

He reminded me an awful lot of my cousin, Sumac, who was very much somewhere between an angel and a cupid.

"Are you my cousin, too?" I demanded, before he could even say anything.

He blinked at me, startled. "No," he said quickly. He frowned. "How did you know that I was an impostor?"

Now that he was speaking in his own voice, I could tell that he had quite a thick accent. It reminded me a little of Justin, Tansy's husband, who was from the Middle Lands, but much thicker. I could still understand him, but the words fell strangely on my ears. It was not an accent I was familiar in associating with my world.

"You're nothing like Timothy," I told him, "even if you were wearing his face. It was... off-putting. Did my father really believe that I would fall for such an obvious ploy?"

His face literally paled at the mention of my father.

I really needed to learn why mentioning him tended to have that effect on people.

"What did my father offer you or threaten you with to get you to play Timothy's part?" I insisted. "What did you hope to accomplish by leading me on?"

He cleared his throat. "I am Caleb of the house of the Griffin. Your father intended that we wed, of course. I am an honorable man and I am in need of a wife." He bent into a stiff position that assumed was supposed to be a bow curtailed by the confines of my rather small car. He grasped both of my hands in his. "Please, my lady," he gasped, "you are fair, and I would give my all to see you happy. Please do not decline my suit so callously."

I actually almost laughed. He was so sweet–so earnest and handsome, but he sounded like a really old romance novel.

It was impossible for me to take him seriously.

"I am flattered," I confessed, "and... almost touched that you would want to marry me after such a brief introduction, but I must decline." I bit my lip, hoping that my words would be enough to keep any more protestations of love, or interest, from pouring from his lips.

He sighed, with all the appearances of being completely crestfallen. "I could only hope," he said.

"You can tell my father to return the real Timothy," I suggested. "He has no right to tell me who I may or may not date."

Caleb grimaced. "No one would dare tell him what he may or may not do," he said ruefully. "Oh, lady, I wish for your sake that you had accepted my troth! I am the first–but I will not be the last, and I fear that I will be the easiest test he has for you."

"I want Timothy," I said bluntly, "and I won't take a cheap imitation. I saw through you–I'll see through whatever else he might have for me." I stared directly into his beautiful green eyes. "You can tell him I said that. He has no right to interfere. No right at all."

By the time I actually managed to convince Caleb to leave and return to wherever the heck he was from, it was dark. I stopped by the bakery to make sure everything was in order, but I fully intended to get home and into a scalding hot tub as fast as I could legally manage.

The shop was all locked up and clean–I could see Iris's hand in the fresh flowers sitting in a vase next to the register. Even the cases were glistening.

I grabbed a trayful of treats and some water bottles for my hairy guy on the doorstep before I left.

"Here you go," I told him, setting them beside him. "And thanks for... earlier. I don't know how you figured it out–but that guy was an impostor. Thanks for trying to look out for me. It's always nice to have a friend."

I thought his eyes actually focused on me for a moment, then he was back to looking through me, towards the night sky.

I sighed.

"Well," I murmured, wishing I had a blanket or something more I could give him, "good night."

Chapter Ten

I whistled happily as I opened the shop a few days later. I had a full day of baking and creating ahead of me and the weather outside was crisp and cool—the perfect combination in my opinion.

Life was pretty good.

I couldn't remember why I had been so stressed out lately. It was funny, but I couldn't think of a single reason why I should be stressed. I was busy, sure, but baking was my bliss.

I set to whipping up a total risk—an avocado lemon pound cake. I'd been flirting with the idea for months, but today seemed like the perfect time to actually test it out.

"Avocado is fruit after all," I reminded myself as I split and pitted the fruit in front of me. "I use avocado oil all the time, why not use the fruit?"

I threw the cubed avocado into my food processor with freshly juiced lemons and set to whipping up my butter and sugar for the base of the pound cake.

Even doing yoga at four in the morning hadn't put a limp in my step. I thought I might actually be getting better at it, under Iris's watchful eyes. Even the well-timed quips from her parrot seemed constructive these days, not irritating.

While the pound cakes cooked in a slow oven I turned my attention to another experiment that had been waiting for me to have the inclination. I dipped fresh bananas into my best churro batter and dropped them into hot lard in the deep fryer. As each one came out, brown and delicious, I sprinkled them liberally with smoked cinnamon and raw sugar.

They were actually quite good.

I'd show Iris how to make them, when she came in with Jessi, and they could make them fresh in the food truck by the order.

The only thing that could make them better was a trio of dipping sauces. Spicy chocolate was a given, I thought, then something citrusy, and, finally, dulce de leche.

Delicioso.

With those two new creations under my belt, I had a big stock of pork rinds to make, as well as candied bacon—in a maple glaze or dark chocolate and sprinkled with sea salt—as well as more date bars to make, a ton of cupcakes, and a whole batch of sticky toffee puddings that my mother had requested I have the twins deliver to her.

She must have been having a tea party or something. I'd never had my mother order anything specifically before. Maybe she was really starting to take my bakery venture seriously.

"Good morning!" I sang as the crew arrived—Iris and Jessi by car and the twins just appearing, as they always did.

This time there was a swirling of dust and Alecto, Jessi's boyfriend appeared, too. Fortunately the dust was of the Magical variety and immediately disappeared. I did not like dirt in my bakery.

"How's everyone today?" I asked, tasting my batter and adding a pinch more cinnamon to the chocolate base. "Isn't the weather just beautiful?"

Everyone just stared at me as if I were crazy.

"You've got to try these banana churros," I told them. "They're seriously good–the bananas get all gooey and yummy inside the deep-fried batter. Don't they taste a little like fried ice cream?"

Starrie nudged Rainey. "What's up with her?" she muttered.

"It's got to be a trap," Rainey answered cautiously. "She's up to something."

I laughed. "Ha! Now you know how it feels to be me–always thinking you're up to something. I'm not, by the way. I'm just in a good mood. I don't know why I've been so stressed out lately."

"You do remember," Jessi said gently, "that the camera crew is coming this afternoon to do your audition for Battling Cupcakes, right?"

I waved her away. "It will be fine," I told her, though in truth I had forgotten.

Oh, well. It was no big deal. It might even be a lot of fun.

Starrie grabbed the box of toffee puddings I had created for my mother. "We'll just deliver these and be right back," she promised. "Let's just hope your insanely good mood rubs off on Mom."

The girls vanished.

"I'm not being that different, am I?" I asked the bemused Iris, who was nibbling on a fried banana with a curious expression on her face.

She grinned. "Yep, it's different. Not different-bad, though. It's nice to see you happy."

"No reason not to be," I quipped. "I'm going to give Hairy Guy some breakfast and then we can start getting ready for the camera crew." I clapped my hands together. "This is pretty exciting, isn't it? I'm going to have to make a lot more cupcakes!"

"Cracked," I thought I heard Jessi whispered. "The pressure's gotten to her at last."

I sat down next to Hairy Guy, giving him a plate of pastries and a big glass of whole milk along with his usual water bottle.

"How are you doing today?" I asked, not even minding when he didn't even look in my direction, but just started crumbling an apple fritter between his fingers before taking a small bite. He glanced in my direction, almost, as he downed half of the milk in one gulp.

I'd have to remember that he really seemed to like milk.

"I have something for you," I told him, going past him to go to my car. I dug into the trunk and brought out the sleeping bag I had bought for him at a camping store down the street. I set it down next to him. "It's water-proof and really warm," I told him. "I don't want you to get too cold at night. It is November, after all, even if we are in Arizona!"

He set a hand on it.

A small part of me thought it would be really nice to hunker down and just hang out with my peaceful friend, but I had a lot of work to do.

"Are you sure you won't come in?" I asked, knowing that he would never answer me. "You wouldn't be in the way at all. If you want... I could even give you a job. I can always use another set of hands."

His head turned in my direction, but his eyes never focused on me.

I didn't know if he even understood what I was trying to say. So many Magical creatures, as I still figured he had to be, didn't speak English at all.

"Well, think about it," I told him. "I'll bring you more food... and a change of clothes, OK?"

Somehow I knew that Hairy Guy had my back. I couldn't think of any reason that I should feel that way, but I just knew that he would try to protect me from anyone who would try to harm me in any way.

He'd never done anything to make me feel protected. I just knew I was.

He was like my very own furry guardian angel.

Rainey and Starrie were back from their errand and working away making cinnamon rolls by the time I got inside. I went straight to my pink mixer, which always made me think about Tansy, and started making a batch of my most popular Miranda cupcakes. They were my best bet to impress the Battling Cupcakes crew.

"What's this audition going to be like?" I asked Jessi, as I mixed the familiar components together. I could have made Miranda cupcakes in my sleep at this point. I made them every day, after all.

Jessi shook her head, her beautiful halo of hair making an aureole around her head. "I have no idea. I think they're just going to taste a couple of your cupcakes and interview you – to see how you come across on camera or something."

I grinned. "Think I should clean up?" I already had flour all over my face, I knew. I just wasn't one of those people that could stay neat while baking.

"I don't think they can handle the real you, yet," Iris laughed. "I brought you a change of clothes and some makeup. Don't worry, Jessi and I will make you a little more presentable."

"We could help," Starrie offered.

"No way," we answered in a chorus.

Chapter Eleven

The crew they sent for the audition was a single woman and a man with a camera. I smiled at them nervously as they peeked into every niche and cranny of the bakery and ate nibbles out of the stacks of cupcakes I had prepared and Iris had painstakingly made gorgeous.

"Hmm," the woman said, rather noncommittally. The camera man focused his lens on me.

I started to sweat.

"Tell me why you should be on Battling Cupcakes," the woman said. "Don't look at me, just look straight into the lens of the camera."

I nodded, licking my lips nervously.

"Breathe," the camera man said with an encouraging smile before disappearing behind his monster of a camera again.

"My name is Cindy Eller," I said, grasping for anything to say. "I should be on Battling Cupcakes because my cupcakes are unique, decadent, and exotic. I use flavor profiles that have never been used before, especially a lot of local flavors."

After that point I had no idea what I was saying. I just knew I had to keep on talking.

"OK." The woman clapped her hands as I floundered to a stop. "That's a wrap."

"It is?" I asked, dumbfounded. "Um, I guess we'll hear from you?"

She shook her head. "No need. You're on the show." She handed me a stack of papers. "Fill these out and fax them to me. We'll see you on set."

I stared after them as they left the bakery, as briskly as they had come in.

"Well," I said, breathlessly. "I guess I'm going to be on TV."

"See?" Jessi said, encouragingly. "I told you that it wasn't going to be a big deal."

Big deal? I felt like someone had left me in the industrial dishwasher for a few cycles!

"What a life!" I sighed, as I turned to get back to work and a multitude of pork rinds to get marinating overnight. I grinned. "Does it get any better than this?"

"You could try dating," Starrie quipped, pulling a tray of cupcakes out of the oven to start cooling.

I frowned. "I don't know if that's a good idea," I told her. "After all—" I paused. I couldn't remember what I had been going to say.

"Yeah, dating doesn't work for Cindy," Rainey teased. "Every guy ends up... huh. Why don't you date, anyway, Cindy?"

I frowned. "I can't think of a good reason. I guess... I've always been too busy?"

"That must be it," Jessi said doubtfully. "It doesn't sound quite right, though. I can't put my finger on it."

I shrugged. "It's not important."

With Iris happily at the helm, I was actually able to go home at a decent time. I gave Merlin a big cuddle, sweeping him into my arms as I got myself together for a little night-time spoiling. I poured a dollop of my favorite bubble mix into my new garden tub and let it fill and froth up as I gathered together a good book–and a pint of ice cream.

I stood in the doorway of the freezer for a long moment.

Why on earth was looking at pints of some random kind of ice cream making me feel so blue, all of a sudden? I didn't even recognize the brand. It was called 'SweetDreams'.

I shrugged it off. Maybe I just wasn't in the mood for ice cream.

I was overdue for a little pampering. I couldn't wait to soak my yoga-sore muscles and actually read a little paranormal romance instead of being too busy planning my next day to do anything special for myself.

Merlin perched next to the tub as I climbed in and eased into the achingly hot water with a hiss of delightful pain/pleasure. He dipped his paw into the water and flicked it out back again, spraying my book with water droplets.

"Nice," I told my cat. "You are so lucky that I prefer a nice paperback when I'm in the tub. If this had been my ereader you would be in huge trouble right now."

Merlin purred contentedly. He knew that I would never punish him.

I was so whipped. I was wrapped around a fat cat's fuzzy tail.

Maybe my sisters were right. Maybe I was missing out on a big part of life, being here with my cat instead of out there in the dating world.

Deep down, I guessed I believed in true love with that one special person. Not a Prince Charming, like Tansy's husband, of course, but a love that was truly meant for me.

I frowned, trying to remember their wedding. For the life of me, I couldn't remember anything about it. My brain was so foggy that I could barely remember Tansy at all–and I had lived with her for a year!

"Ugh," I told Merlin. "I swear, I'm getting old. My brain is all kinds of foggy today."

Merlin just purred sleepily from the side of the tub. He was dangling his paw into the water again.

"You should get in," I told him. "The water is wonderful."

He opened his eyes just a slit to regard me coolly. It was as plain as day that he was telling me that cats did not take bubble baths.

"You'd love it," I insisted. "Cats are all about spoiling themselves, right?"

My familiar just closed his eyes and pretending to sleep.

That wasn't a bad idea, I decided.

I closed my eyes and let myself drift off to dreamland.

I awoke with a keen sense of loss. I couldn't remember my dreams, but there were tears on my cheeks when I touched them.

Something wasn't right. I couldn't my finger on it, but I knew I was missing a piece–a huge piece of my life.

That's what I got for falling asleep reading a romance novel.

Despite myself, I couldn't shake the feeling off.

I dragged myself out of the much-cooler tub and dried off, racking my brain, trying to figure out what it was that was making my mind feel so... itchy.

"What am I forgetting?" I asked. "Why do I feel like there's a huge chunk of my brain missing?"

Merlin had abandoned me while I was sleeping. I got into my pajamas and decided to watch a little TV. There was nothing like a good old documentary to make me feel sleepy again.

I flipped the TV in the family room on and scanned through the channels. There was only one documentary on at this hour of the night.

"What is wrong with me?" I demanded, moments later. "Why on earth should a show about toads make me cry?"

Chapter Twelve

All the next day I was out of sorts.

I couldn't get past the feeling that I was missing something big. Every time I tried to sort it out my head would start aching until I felt like I was going to be sick.

And I kept seeing toads everywhere. I mean, it was winter in Arizona! The toads were all hibernating! So, why was I seeing toy toads at the store? And why on earth would I have so many toad molds in the bakery?

Why couldn't I remember having toad truffles and why was everyone ordering them?

I kind of felt like tearing my hair out by the roots.

"I feel like I got up on the wrong side of the universe today," I told Jessi, when I actually managed to burn a whole batch of Miranda cupcakes—something that never happened to me. "I need a break. I'm going to take Hairy Guy some coffee cake and hot chocolate. Don't call me unless you have to."

Jessi nodded, her face full of concern.

I didn't blame her. My face in the mirror this morning had been pinched and piqued, with huge dark circles under my eyes. I couldn't remember my dreams, but I remembered dreaming, and I had woken up even more exhausted than when I had gone to sleep.

"Today sucks," I told Hairy Guy as I gave him his food.

As usual he had nothing to say in return, but that was OK. I always felt like he was listening, even if he never looked straight at me.

I rubbed my temples. Just trying to think was starting to give me a migraine.

"I need to talk to Stephan," I told Hairy. "Maybe I've got some kind of Magical flu."

It was my day for visiting Stephan and getting some help with my rather capricious Magic. I didn't really remember how we had come to such an agreement, but I was always grateful to have someone to turn to when something went Magically awry.

My head was really pounding by the time I made it through the portal and past the ghoul doorman at Stephan's club. I'd never had such a bad headache in my entire life.

My stepfather had tea ready, as always, and offered me a steaming cup. I inhaled the ginger-infused fumes, feeling a minute releasing of the agony in my head.

"I feel like my head was run over by a herd of pegasi," I told him, sipping at the hot liquid. "Are there any Magical maladies going on at the moment that you know about?"

He frowned, shaking his head. "Not that I know of," he admitted, offering me a plate of my very own tea cakes.

"No thanks," I sighed, leaning back in my customary chair. "I feel so foggy—like I can't even think."

Stephan's frown deepened. "And you think it's a Magical problem?"

I shrugged. "I don't really know. It just doesn't feel... right."

Stephan pursed his lips, his dimples popping into view underneath his short beard.

Dimples.

The pain roared through my body.

Dimples.

A handsome face.

Ice cream.

A tiny toad on my collar.

A real first kiss.

Timothy.

I clenched my fists as the pain came shooting down on me again, trying to force the fog back down on my brain.

"I'm not going to forget Timothy!" I shouted. "I love him! You can't make me forget he ever existed!"

The pain lingered only a moment longer.

Then it was gone.

I could breathe again.

Stephan stared up at me, his eyebrows raised and mouth open. "Care to explain what just happened?"

I rubbed my head. The pain was completely gone. "My father," I spat. "I didn't fall for his little trick, so he tried to make me forget Timothy altogether." I fought the urge to chuck my teacup at something. Stephan's set was too valuable to waste to my temper.

"I'm not going to take this lying down," I growled instead. "I'm going to figure out some way to make my father pay for interfering like this. He has no business messing with my life!"

Stephan actually laughed.

I stared at him.

He shook his head apologetically. "Sometimes you really do remind me of your mother," he murmured.

I wasn't sure whether to take that as a compliment or a criticism.

I gripped the arms of my chair with my fingers. "I need to prove to my father that he can't just act like this, but how? How do I tell…" I bit my lip, realizing that I was bordering on betraying what I knew of my father from Sumac–something I didn't have the authority to disclose.

"Someone in Faerie," Stephan supplied helpfully, smoothly covering my near faux pas. "I can't imagine how you would manage that."

I scowled. "I'll think of something," I said darkly. "He'll rue the day he decided to fiddle around with my life."

Stephan stifled another chuckle against his tea cup.

I settled back to drink my own tea, my mind already focused on my revenge. The sharpness of the ginger in the tea was mellowed just enough by a touch of peppermint.

I really needed to start using that flavor combination at the shop. It was really good.

I blinked, frowning at my teacup.

Ginger and peppermint?

And… dates and bacon?

I nibbled on my bottom lip, regarding my stepfather who was suddenly ignoring me quite studiously.

"Stephan," I said slowly. "Is my mother… pregnant?"

Chapter Thirteen

Stephan's ears turned red.

I set my teacup down and kept my eyes on his face.

"Well?" I prompted.

My stepfather fumbled with his own cup, spilling tea all over himself and the table. He mopped it up with a handkerchief, avoiding my eyes.

I cleared my throat, raising my eyebrows pointedly.

"Yes," he admitted, "but we weren't going to tell anyone yet."

I sighed. "How did this happen? Never mind. I know how it happened. Ew. I don't need to have that image in my mind, thank you very much. Seriously? You two are pregnant?"

"This is going well," Stephan murmured, folding his handkerchief fastidiously and putting it to the side.

I frowned in thought. "This is all Sumac's fault!" I realized. "Her stupid cupid Magic! Everyone I know is pregnant right now." I looked up at my stepfather. "You do know that Rose is also knocked up?"

He winced at my word choice, but nodded.

"Well," I said wryly. "Congratulations, Daddy."

His eyebrows shot up in surprise.

"Unless you prefer to be called 'Papa'?" I suggested. "This is your first kid, isn't it?"

He nodded mutely.

Poor guy, it must be quite a shock for him. He was closer to seventy than to fifty and he was becoming a 'real' father for the first time? Not that it was unheard of in the Magical Community–witches tended to live longer and stay younger, so it was perfectly reasonable for my mother to have another child. They wouldn't even be considered late in life parents.

I just hadn't seen that one coming, somehow.

I was going to have a nephew or a niece and a sister or brother that were the same age.

Wow.

"This spell you just broke," Stephan interrupted my thoughts, munching thoughtfully on a tea cake. "It was pretty... huge, wasn't it?"

I nodded, frowning as I thought about it. "He tried to erase every single aspect of my life that might remind me of Timothy–which is why I couldn't think–he erased my toad kissing days, even my favorite brand of ice cream!" I shook my head. "And it wasn't just me, either. Everyone I talked to the last couple days seemed to have their memories wiped out as well–that must have taken a huge amount of power!"

"A prodigious amount," Stephan agree, "which has now most likely snapped right back on the person who cast it."

I stared at him.

He gave me a tiny smile. "I would say that was quite a powerful revenge, wouldn't you?"

I almost winced in sympathy–but not quite. That much backlash could really cause a lot of damage. Even a small spell, interrupted, could result in horrible burns.

I remembered one particular time when I had tried to help my mother in her garden, only to have the spell snap back and catch me in the backlash. I'd burned my hands so badly they had blistered.

And that was only a tiny little spell, meant to attract ladybugs. I hadn't been trying to change someone's whole memory–and not even close to trying to erase a whole person from everyone's memories.

"Ouch," I muttered. "That's going to leave a mark."

Stephan nodded. "If my guess is correct," he said, "your father will be in no position to hassle you Magically for some time."

"That," I said, "is the best news I've heard in a long time."

I returned to a bakery in chaos.

On the surface everything was business as usual–calm and peaceful, but the worst thing I could have imagined had happened.

My mother was there.

And she had seen Iris.

When I walked through the door, Starrie and Rainey were studiously chopping dates up by hand, when they could have just as easily used the food processor. I noticed that they both had their heads down. They had enough self-preservation not to want to be part of this showdown.

And I had stepped right into the line of fire.

"Mother," I exclaimed. "What are you doing here?"

She turned to stare at me, her lips pursed in irritation. "I came to get a box of pastries," she said, "and then I find out that all of you have been lying to me!"

To my absolute consternation she burst into tears.

Outside it began to sprinkle, which wouldn't have been an issue if there were even a single cloud in the sky.

"Mom!" I protested, knowing that it was up to me, as usual, to save the day. I put my arm around her. "Don't cry," I said. "We weren't lying to you. We just wanted to surprise you... Iris and I are going to be on Battling Cupcakes together!"

She sniffed, "But she left her job," she said, drawing in a deep breath. "Her wonderful, beautiful architecture job to come work at a *bakery* !"

"At the family business," I reminded her, trying not to feel slighted by her tone when she was talking about my livelihood and passion.

She did seem to brighten a little at that thought.

Which just turned the waterworks on worse. The sprinkle outside turned into a downpour. "All my girls," she sobbed, "working together... it's just so beautiful!" Her bottom lip trembled. "Finally you work together and it has to be at a *bakery* ?"

"She's pregnant," I explained to my sisters, Jessi, and the two customers waiting in line that were starting to look a little nervous.

"We know," everyone said.

I put my hands on my hips as I stared at my mother. "They know?" I demanded. "Why didn't you tell *me* ?"

"Well, duh," Starrie said. "We live with her."

"Yeah," Rainey echoed. "Of course we knew. Why do you think we wanted a job? We couldn't stay home with that." She gestured towards my mother, who was scrubbing at her eyes with a tissue.

I narrowed my eyes at Iris.

"Well," she said uncomfortably. "Come on. If you hadn't been so distracted lately you would have realized what was going on a lot sooner. I mean, all the signs were there. Dates and bacon? Sticky toffee pudding? When does our mother eat like that if she's not pregnant?"

"So, does everyone know except for me?" I demanded.

"You're so busy," my mother said, pulling herself together with a conscious effort. "I didn't want to pull you away from your oh-so important bakery work."

Great, now I felt inadequate and guilty. I didn't know how she did that.

"Mom," I said, trying not to let my frustration touch my voice. "You know that family always comes first. I'm never too busy for you. You know that! You should have told me!"

My mother sniffed. "As you told me about Iris quitting her entire future in Architecture? It seems that I'm not the only one withholding information."

Touché.

"Mom," Iris interjected gently. "I need to do this. I promise—if I don't make it as an artist in a year I will go back and finish my PH.D. It's all cleared with my advisor. It's just a leave of absence, OK?"

My mother considered that for a moment before nodding. "Despite what you may think," she said stiffly. "I only want what's best for you. Maybe this year will help you get your head on straight and help you to see where your true success would lie."

She brightened suddenly. "You can design the baby's room! We'll have to build a new wing onto the house."
Iris sighed.

Chapter Fourteen

I sent my mother away with a dozen sticky toffee puddings and set to work, trying to distract myself from the realization that my father still had Timothy in his clutches.

Despite Sumac's reassurance to the contrary, I was terrified that he would do something to harm my boyfriend. After all, he had no compunction against erasing Timothy's existence from my life.

I frowned as I started the long process zesting a basketful of limes for my new mango-lime meringue pie. Creating something finicky, like a curd, was exactly what I needed to distract myself. The tangy scent of citrus filled the air, helping to clear my head and get me to relax.

I'd always loved the flavor of mango and lime together. Already my mouth was watering at the thought of the tart, tropical curd paired with a mass of fluffy white meringue clouds. It was going to be insanely delicious.

Rainey and Starrie appeared over my shoulders as they realized that I was creating a new recipe.

Rainey pulled out a little notepad and started taking notes, while Starrie pursed her lips and watched me with narrowed eyes.

"I'm going to make Mango-Meringue tarts," I explained as I put my double boiler onto the stove to heat up the ingredients for the curd. "The crust is going to be based in pistachios and macadamia nuts and there's going to be a lot of lime in the curd to give it some tanginess. The meringue is sweet enough on its own, so the tarts are going to need that lime to brighten them up."

I handed Starrie the whisk as I added the fruit juice and sugar to the pan. "Keep stirring this as it thickens," I told her. "Once you know how to make a simple curd you can start playing with flavors—like blackberries or tangerine... pretty much anything you can think of."

"What about chocolate?" she asked.

I pursed my lips, considering. "It's pretty much the same thing—you just use milk or cream with the cocoa instead of juice and zest."

She nodded, her face shifting to the expression I was used to associating with one of her schemes. Creativity was flowing behind those moon-silver eyes of hers. "What about," she said slowly, "a jalapeno raspberry pie?"

I grinned, impressed. "That is an awesome idea, Star!"

She actually blushed. "Well, you made us all jam last year for Christmas and my favorite was the raspberry-jalapeno jelly."

Rainey nodded. "She put it on everything." She made a face. "Literally... everything."

"Well, then," I said with a laugh, "I'll have to teach you how to make the jelly sometime. Meanwhile we can see what there is to create with the few jars I have left."

"Cheesecake," Rainey suggested.

"Cake filling for a birthday cake?" Starrie suggested uncertainly.

I gave her a squeeze. "If you keep coming up with ideas like this I will have to hire you on a permanent basis."

This time her ultra-pale skin turned a brilliant pink.

"What about..." Rainey said thoughtfully. "A cheesecake with pears, honey, and goat cheese?"

I blinked at her.

"You girls," I told them, "are starting to think like real pastry chefs!"

In the end, we made all of those things and more–including truffles using the jalapeno-raspberry cheesecake and pear goat cheese ideas as fillings.

When the chocolate ganache shells were done hardening, Iris showed them how to decorate the truffles.

I'd never seen them look happier.

"I'm going to put a notebook on the counter," I announced. "Any time anyone gets an idea I want you to write it down in there, OK?"

Starrie popped a spicy jalapeno raspberry truffle in her mouth with a grin. "Can you teach us how to make jam?" she suggested.

I pursed my lips. "It's a huge job," I admitted. "I guess we can... as long as we plan ahead. I'll need all hands on deck."

Both girls nodded.

"That will have to wait," Jessi announced, appearing from the register with a stack of papers. "I just got your itinerary for Battling Cupcakes."

I licked my lips. Just thinking about the competition made my mouth feel dry. "When?" I managed to squeak.

"Three days from now," Jessi announced. "You and Iris need to get yourselves to California for the filming."

"What about the bakery?" I protested. "I can't be gone for three whole days!"

"We can handle it," Starrie said stoutly.

"Yeah," Rainey agreed. "We can handle it for a couple days. We have all your recipes. We know how to follow instructions."

I frowned at her doubtfully.

"Think of the bakery," Jessi said dramatically, putting her arm around my shoulders. "Think of the publicity!"

"Unless I crash and burn," I muttered. "Anyway, how am I going to hide my Magic? You can't do it if you're here and I'm there."

Starrie rolled her eyes.

"Can you?" I squeaked.

"Well, duh," the twins chorused.

"Morrigan Magic," Iris murmured.

That was not a reassuring thought at all. Morrigan Magic was... mischievous at best and skirted dark Magic at worst.

"No funny business, OK?" I said nervously.

The twins looked far too innocent to make me feel better.

"Relax," Starrie suggested.

"Yeah," Rainey added soothingly. "What's the worst that could happen?"

I shuddered. I could imagine far too many scenarios of absolute disaster. I mean, I was putting myself in the hands of the twins.

I must be losing my mind.

Iris clapped her hands. "We should get packed!" she enthused. "We have to decide what we're going to wear. I can't believe we're going to be on TV." She eyed me. "Do you have anything that isn't black?"

"Nope," I told her.

"You can get something from my closet," Jessi said soothingly, to my dismay.

"Hey," I protested. "I like my clothes."

"They're boring," Iris announced. "Sad and drab." She heaved a sigh dramatically, her eyes glinting with excitement. She reached up her hand to touch Chloe, where the tiny bat was clinging to her ear like a cuff. "I guess I have some shopping to do before we go!"

"Nothing too... sparkly!" I called after her, but she was already gone in a glimmer of rainbow colors.

"Face it," Starrie told me sympathetically, putting her hand on my arm, "you're going to be dazzling."

"Seriously," Rainey agreed.

I sighed. I was just going to have to face the facts. "Yeah. I know."

Chapter Fifteen

The day before we left for California was an absolute madhouse.

"There's no way I can leave," I moaned to Jessi as the tenth werewolf order of pork rinds came in all within an hour. "There's just too much to get done here."

"It will be fine," Jessi told me briskly, handing out yet another box of cupcakes. Business was booming today. "Alecto and I will keep the twins in line."

I grimaced. "Jessi—"

She shook her head. "We can handle it," she insisted.

Alecto appeared beside her and grinned down at me from his towering height. The D'jinn had a smile that just oozed charm—his very white teeth gleaming in his darkly handsome face.

Ugh. I just didn't trust him at all.

"Relax," he suggested in his velvety smooth voice. "With Jessi in charge, what can go wrong?"

Jessi beamed under the praise.

I sighed. He had a point. "OK," I conceded as I piped cinnamon cream-cheese frosting onto a pumpkin-maple cupcake. "I trust you, Jessi. I know you won't let anything fall apart."

Alecto winked at Jessi and disappeared again into the back of the shop. She shook her head as she looked after him.

"Jessi–" I started again.

She held up her hand. "I know what you're going to say," she said, "and I'm going to stop you. I can handle Alecto, Cindy. I know you don't think I can, but it's under control. I promise."

I bit my lip. "I guess it's none of my business anyway," I admitted.

"Hey," Jessi squeezed my shoulder. "I really appreciate you caring enough to want to protect me. It's nice to know you've got my back, even if I think you are wrong about Alecto."

"Fair enough." I handed her a cupcake.

She bit into it with a grin. "Gosh, I love pumpkin," she murmured around the crumbs. "Especially when you put chai in the filling. Seriously, Cindy, if I get fat I am going to hate you!"

I grinned. There was no sign of any extra weight on Jessi's long and lean frame. I didn't think she needed to worry about my cupcakes.

Jessi frowned, looking past me. "Um, Cindy?" she cleared her throat. "What's going on with Iris today?"

I turned to see what Jessi was looking at.

Iris sat quietly at the counter, painting my rose-strawberry cupcakes black.

Starrie tittered, passing with an order of pork rinds for a member of what we were calling 'Sumac's baby boom'. "What goes up..." she whispered.

"... must come down," I finished. "Oh... pooh."

Jessi's eyebrows rose. "What?" she asked.

"Iris," I explained. "She's been so up lately it was bound to happen. She's on the downswing now."

"Downswing," Jessi repeated. "So... painting roses black?"

I nodded. "Followed by sad music, the reading of tragedies, and lots of dark art."

Jessi bit her lip. "How long...?"

I shrugged. "With Iris you never can tell. It could last a day... or a week."

Jessi winced.

"Yeah," I agreed. "Do you still think Battling Cupcakes is a good idea?"

"Sure," Jessi said positively. "I mean, she's still amazingly talented, even if the roses are black instead of pink. I'm positive you guys will still do a great job."

She was good. She almost had me convinced that she actually believed it.

Too bad I could read the uncertainty in her eyes.

The bell over the door rang and Amy swept in. I'd heard of the pregnancy glow, of course, but I had never actually seen it in action. All the pregnant women I had spent time around were more the 'glistening from sweat and misery' type.

Amy was actually glowing. Her long blond hair shone like rippling sunshine. Her skin was a burnished pale gold. So far she hadn't put on a single pound that I could see.

She looked majestic.

"You look fantastic," I told her as I packaged up her pork rinds. "Pregnancy really agrees with you."

She beamed. "That's so sweet of you!" She clasped her hands together. "We finally know why I'm getting so huge! We think it's going to be twins!"

"Twins?" I blinked. "Wow. Congratulations. That's amazing!"

She nodded. "And, of course, I'm going to need you to cater my baby shower. It's going to be huge." She pushed her sunglasses back on her head. "After what you did for my wedding, I know you won't let me down!"

I swallowed as I nodded. Any catering for Amy was a huge job.

"I'll be back with the details," she promised as she took her bakery box. She blew kisses to everyone and disappeared back out of the door.

"Looks like we're in the baby shower business," I told Jessi.

She rubbed her hands together. "Excellent."

I laughed. "As long as I can leave the organizing up to you and just handle the baking myself, we're good!"

"Actually," Jessi teased, "I thought we should change things up. You can organize events and I'll doing the cooking from now on."

I shuddered. "Ha. Ha. You're so funny, Jessi."

She giggled. "As if I could cook anything without burning it. I'm useless in the kitchen."

"Well," I hesitated, "not completely useless."

The bell rang over the door again. Jessi and I both turned to greet the customer.

The tall, handsome man took two steps into the bakery and gazed into my eyes. He dropped to one knee and opened up his arms dramatically.

"My lady–" he started.

"Out!" I commanded, crossing the counter to grab his collar. I yanked hard until he came up off of his knees. "Get out!"

Jessi stared as I less than gently removed the man from my shop. I may or may not have used a little Magic to help him along.

"What was that?" she demanded as I returned, dusting off my hands.

"My father," I said darkly, "seems to have recovered a lot faster than I was hoping."

"Your father sends you hot guys who throw themselves at your feet?" Jessi demanded. "Seriously? Can we trade dads? Mine just gives me really good advice."

"My father," I told her, "doesn't approve of my choice in a boyfriend."

Jessi looked at me blankly. "What's wrong with Timothy–other than the fact that he's been MIA?"

"He's not MIA," I said. "My father did something to him. Why? Because Timothy is an Ordinary."

"Wait," Jessi said. "I thought you didn't know anything about your father."

"It's all that stuff I'm not supposed to tell you," I said. "My father is some kind of big honcho..." I lowered my voice. "In Faerie."

Jessi's eyes widened. "Wow," she said with a laugh. "Really?"

"What?" I asked, narrowing my eyes at her as she continued to laugh.

Jessi giggled. "You're some real live freakin' fairy princess?"

I couldn't tell Jessi that it was more like I was the daughter of a god. I'd already told her more than I should have.

"Something like that," I agreed, "and it seriously sucks. I liked it better before I knew anything about him."

"Dads can be a pain in the ass," Jessi agreed. She twisted one of the many bracelets on her arm. "So... when are you going to meet him?"

"My dad?" I demanded. "Never, I hope!"

Chapter Sixteen

The whole long drive to California I couldn't help but think about Jessi's assumption that I would want to meet my biological father.

The thought had never really crossed my mind.

After all, he was some stranger in Faerie that kept messing with my life–first by sending Sumac to spy on me and now trying to get me married off to some random Magical guy who he could keep under his thumb.

I didn't know one good thing about my father, other than that my mother said she still loved him. The fact that she had bound my Magic to keep him from finding me for twenty-five years did not make me feel any better about that.

It wasn't like meeting my father was even an option. Faerie was forbidden territory–the unknown. I was the offspring of an absolutely taboo relationship. I didn't even know what I was capable of Magically because of that heritage.

No one knew what I was capable of and that was frightening.

My whole life I had been different. My mother had bound my Magic because she was afraid that my father might find me and take me away. Because of that, I had never had any real abilities, other than baking, until recently, and I still felt a little wary about trying anything new. I had spent years doing nothing more than baking cupcakes and turning men into toads, wondering why I was such a failure of a witch.

It sucked.

"Iris," I said to my sister, who was leaning back in the passenger seat of my car, staring glumly out of the window, her hoodie pulled up to hide her rainbow-faceted hair, "do you have a good relationship with your father?"

Iris blinked at me, startled by the question. She, like all my sisters, had been raised primarily by my mother. Unlike me, though, she knew who her dad was.

"My dad," Iris said thoughtfully. "Yeah, I guess we have a good relationship. He can be kind of... self-obsessed sometimes, but the rest of the time he's a really cool guy. Why?"

"Nothing important," I told her. "I've just been thinking about my dad a lot lately."

I had my sister's full attention now. "That's right," she said, "you're the only one of us who never really had a dad."

"I've had a lot of dads," I said with a laugh. "I've had all of your dads and some. I just don't know much about my biological father."

In fact, I wasn't sure when it had happened, but I had started to look to Stephan as a father figure. I hadn't known him for a really long time, but I already had a better relationship with him than I had with any of my other stepfathers. I really respected and admired him, too. If that didn't make him the perfect father for me, I didn't know what would.

"My dad," Iris said thoughtfully, "is brilliant, temperamental, and artistic... everything that Mom has tried to rein in on me. Who knows, maybe she is right. I'll never make it as an artist anyway."

"Your dad does," I pointed out.

Iris shrugged and heaved a deep sigh. "That doesn't mean that I can."

"Look," I told her. "I know that it will sound to you like I'm just being your big sister, but I know that you have a future as an artist–if that's what you want to do. You're extremely talented. Look at what you did in the house–that mural in your room is breathtaking!"

Iris shrugged again. "I don't know."

"Well, I do," I said positively. "The only thing that stands in the way of your ambitions and dreams is you. Don't let Mom or anyone else tell you otherwise. I know you're not a quitter."

Her lips turned up slightly. She brushed back a strand of her rainbow-colored hair that had escaped from her hood. "Thanks, sis. By the way, it does sound like you're just being a big sister, but I still appreciate it."

I grinned. "Let's have fun with this, OK? When was the last time we had the opportunity to spend this much together, just the two of us?"

Iris smiled almost shyly. "Never."

I nodded. "Exactly. Let's have fun–go to the beach, hang out..."

"Make cupcakes," she interjected.

I shrugged. "Sure. Why not? I guess we could do that too."

Iris actually giggled.

"Aren't you worried about tomorrow?" she asked. "I mean, being in front of the cameras and everything?"

I glanced at her. "Is that what's bothering you? All the cameras and everything?"

She shrugged. "I've never been on TV before."

"Me neither," I admitted. "We'll both be trying something new."

"Aren't you nervous?" she insisted. "I feel like I'm going to throw up."

"Of course I'm nervous," I admitted. "I'm extremely nervous, actually. I just show it differently than you do."

"You don't show it at all," she said. She sighed, looking out of her window at the passing scenery. "What if I let you down, Cindy? What if I mess up and we lose?"

"What if I mess up?" I countered. "What if I burn down the whole set?"

Iris giggled. "You never burn anything."

I grinned. "Well, what if I do? What if everything is a whole disaster? So what?"

Iris shrugged. "I don't know."

"Me neither," I agreed. "I don't know if it will affect business or if nothing will change. All I know is that I'm going to do my best to bake some good cupcakes... even if they give me something truly disgusting to work with... like durian! I honestly don't see how you could mess this up. You're an incredible artist."

"I always mess up," she said in a small voice.

I actually stared at her for a moment. "What on earth are you talking about?"

Iris shrugged. "Everything I do ends up in complete disaster," she said in a voice barely louder than a whisper. "That's the real reason why I quit my architecture program–it was going so well that I knew it was going to bomb."

"But Iris," I protested. "You couldn't know that!"

She shrugged. "It always happens with me. Do you remember when I was a kid and Mom let me plant that whole corner of the garden any way I wanted?"

I nodded.

"Well, you don't know this, but everything was really beautiful for about a week... and then it all just suddenly shriveled up and died. Mom had to replant everything and start from scratch. She never let me touch her garden again."

"Iris," I started, "I'm sure that was just a coincidence–"

"But it's not!" she protested. "That time the twins asked to me to watch their chickens for them... they started laying rocks, Cindy! Rocks!"

"Iris," I tried to interrupt.

"I tried to hatch out a butterfly and it went rogue and ate my whole bedroom!" she shouted. "And that mural in my room? Well, last night it came to life and drenched everything! I had to chase a panther around the house for an hour!"

I turned to stare at her long enough that she shrieked and slammed my hands back onto the steering wheel.

"You see?" she whispered. "I'm the very last person that should be going with you to Battling Cupcakes. If I had been on the Titanic there wouldn't have been any survivors." My little sister crouched further into her seat as if she could make herself disappear.

"Stop talking like that," I told her. "Maybe the whole problem is your attitude. You know that believing something like that can be its own jinx. That's what ended up being the problem with me and all those men turning into toads... it was because I had a deeply rooted belief that all men were toads."

Iris sighed as she shook her head. "I knew you wouldn't believe me, Cindy. No one ever does. But you'll see, I'm like Murphy's Law come to life... everything is going to go wrong tomorrow. It's guaranteed."

Chapter Seventeen

"Three. Two. One."

The lights on the set were hot and blinding. Underneath the sparkly black tank top Iris had bought for me I was already starting to sweat and filming hadn't even started yet.

"Welcome to Battling Cupcakes," Owen Dark, the host announced, grinning cheesily into the camera trained on him. On TV he always looked great, but in person it was a bit too much. "Today we have an extra-special treat for you." He gestured behind him. "But please let me introduce our judges first. Candy Joyce, international pastry superstar coming to us from her world-famous Bakery, Lard. Next to her is our second judge, Zachery Jeffries, International renowned Chocolatier and pastry instructor. Next we come to our guest judge–a man whose desserts are considered to be nothing short of Magical–Mr. Devon Kane!"

I heard Iris let out her breath in a hiss next to me. I knew she, too, was seeing the aura of power around this guest judge–he was Magical! Not only that, but he was staring at both of us steadily.

He knew what we were.

That made two Magical beings I had spotted since entering the set–the first being Owen Dark himself–the guy practically screamed Middle Lander blood.

Iris nudged me and I followed her gaze towards the right and one our own competitors.

Make that three Magical people. The baker's assistant was also surrounded by power.

"D'jinn," Iris murmured in my ear, so softly I almost didn't hear her.

I fought the urge to lick my lips. All I could do was hope that Rainey and Starrie had followed through with their promise to hide my Magic from the cameras. The last thing I needed was to reveal the existence of Magic all over the world on TV.

"As you all know," Owen said, his smarmy grin still focused on the camera, "there are three rounds to this competition. The first round is all about your flavor profiles and creativity when faced with our baskets of doom."

That didn't sound good. I didn't remember it seeming so sinister when I was watching Battling Cupcakes at home. Back at home it had always been a thrill, seeing what they would throw at the bakers.

It was much less fun on this side of the camera.

"The second round, if you make it that far," Owen continued, "is about theme–flavor and decorations are equally essential."

"Round three–the final round–is where two lucky competitors will go head to head to create the perfect display and treats for a special event!"

"Our first round, the creativity and flavor round will begin..." Owen paused dramatically, "Now! Please open your baskets to see the required ingredients for this first round of competition."

My hands were shaking so badly at this point I wasn't even sure if I was going to be able to get the basket open. I took a deep breath and steadied myself for the worst.

"And the mandatory ingredients," Owen announced, "are carob chips, canned peas, parsley, and maple syrup."

I stared down at the ingredients as if they were going to jump out and bite me. Canned peas? Parsley? What was I going to do with stuff like that? For one thing, I found canned peas utterly offensive as a whole–processed and tinny tasting, how was I going to highlight them in any way that would be even remotely palatable?

"OK," I said to Iris as the horn blasted and the round was officially starting. "Peas... parsley... maple syrup. Let's make a carrot cupcake with the peas and parsley in it–we'll add some fresh pineapple to take some of that nasty aluminum flavor out of it."

Iris nodded nervously. "What about the carob chips?"

I pursed my lips. Carob chips were used as a substitute by people who were allergic to chocolate, but I found the flavor to be heavy and on the bitter side. "We'll melt them down and add them to the batter," I decided. "I've made chocolate carrot cake before, this isn't that different. We'll make a maple cream filling and a maple–carob cream cheese frosting. Hopefully this won't be taking the easy way out."

Iris nodded. "I'll start melting the carob chips," she said, rushing off to do so.

I glanced at the clock. I had already wasted a full five minutes trying to come up with a plan. I needed to get the batter made and into the oven as quickly as I could manage.

I found a huge bunch of multi-colored carrots in the fridge and put them through the food processor with pineapple, the parsley, and–wincing–the canned peas. I sniffed at the resulting slurry and decided that I needed something to mellow out the peas even more. I grabbed up a bag of unsalted pistachios and ground them up with carrot mixture.

That smelled a lot better.

I whipped butter and sugar together and started mixing my cupcakes. Iris handed me the melted carob and I added it very slowly to my mixture–I didn't want to cook my batter before it even got into the oven.

Iris scooped the mixture into the cupcake pans and stuck them into the oven as I started working on a whipped cream sweetened with maple syrup for the filling. I wanted it to be a little denser than just cream, so I mixed in some goat cheese. I tasted the mixture and nodded to myself–it was magic!

So far it looked like Rainey and Starrie had been able to keep their word–I was being able to use my Magic, but there were none of the usual sparks and glimmers around me as I was working. I kind of missed them.

I just hoped my Magic was working enough to keep me from burning the cupcakes. I wasn't sure I could ever live down being sent home after the first round.

The time flew by faster than I could believe. The cupcakes came out of the oven and into the fridge to cool enough not to melt the frosting. I finished whipping up the filling and the topping while Iris threw together a cute decoration of a maple leaf for the top of the cupcakes.

She placed the last decoration on the last cake just as the alarm sounded.

Round one was over.

I gulped in a deep breath as I looked over at Iris. "Whew," I told her. "That was intense."

She nodded, staring down at the cupcakes. "What do you think?"

I shook my head nervously. "I have no idea."

Lining up in front of the judges felt an awful lot like standing in front of a firing squad, or at least as I would have imagined that would feel. I was so focused on my cupcakes that I scarcely heard what they said to the baker before me—a cute girl from LA, at least until I heard Devon Kane speak.

"Not good," he told the girl. "These are utterly inedible."

I could feel my heart fluttering around in my ribcage like a distressed dove. I couldn't keep myself from staring at him as he slowly unwrapped my cupcake and took the smallest bite before placing it back on the plate and folding his hands.

"Cindy," Candy said with a sincere smile, "this is certainly a unique cupcake. The texture was good and I definitely picked up on the maple."

I nodded.

"This was a good cupcake," Jeffries announced. "I like the idea of pineapple in the cake to take the edge off of the canned peas."

Then it was Devon Kane's turn. I swallowed as he looked coolly at me.

"I would have liked to taste a little more parsley," was all he said.

I kind of checked out while the other competitors were being critiqued. What did Kane's comment mean? Had he liked my cupcake or not? I couldn't tell. Had my lack of parsley cost me the whole competition?

Had I played it too safe?

We filed out into another room while the judges deliberated. Iris handed me an icy water bottle and I downed it in one long gulp.

"Well?" she asked quietly.

I shook my head. "I have no idea. I couldn't tell if they liked the cupcake or not."

"Canned peas," Iris said in disgust. "That's just disgusting."

I smiled at her. "I know, right? Either someone sick and twisted came up with that basket, or someone really didn't like our judges."

"Maybe both," Iris giggled.

The door opened and we were ushered out to face the judges.

"The judges felt only one of you truly captured the appropriate balance of flavors," Owen said with a toothy grin aimed towards the camera. "However, one of you was unable to create a cupcake with all of the ingredients in a form that was, well... edible. I'm sorry, Georgia, but this battle is over for you."

I let my breath out in a gush, feeling a little faint.

We had done it.

We were still in the competition.

Chapter Eighteen

The relief I felt at making it to the second round was quickly replaced with raw nerves and abject terror. I had barely made it through–how was I going to survive another round?

Owen Dark was already talking again, the charm flying fast and thick. "Bakers," he said, "are you ready for the second round? Remember, this round is fifty percent decoration and fifty percent flavor–all based on our inspiration." He waved his arms towards a towering curtain behind us dramatically. "Today's inspiration is..."

I gulped nervously.

"Snow!" Owen chortled as flakes of fake plastic snow fluttered over our heads and got tangled in my hair. "Design and create three delicious cupcakes in this theme starting... Now!"

We raced for our kitchens.

"Snow?" I whispered to Iris. "How can I design three cupcakes around *snow* ?"

She pursed her lips, shaking her head.

"White," I murmured, "cold... fluffy. Well, I'll have to make my coconut-lime cream cake, right?"

Iris nodded. "I'll make fondant six-fold symmetry snowflakes with a little sparkle for the top," she suggested.

I nodded. "Perfect. Now... what about something cold?"

Iris wrinkled her nose. "Cold? How are you going to manage something like that?"

I bit my fingernail, looking over at the corner where the ice cream machine was looming.

"Ice cream?" Iris hissed. "Are you crazy? No one ever uses the ice cream machine on Battling Cupcakes. It is the siren of doom."

"An ice cream cupcake would be perfect," I hissed back. "I'm going to go for it. I'll make a... pineapple gelato for the filling of a mango cupcake with a little spicy dulce de leche whipped cream frosting."

Iris nodded. "Sounds great," she agreed. "What about the third?"

"I have to do chocolate," I told her, "something dark and decadent, but with a creamy frosting–like a snow capped mountain."

Iris nodded again.

"Can you handle the decorations?" I asked her.

She nodded, smiling a little grimly. I could see the determination shining in her dark eyes. "I can do this," she promised.

We bumped fists and got to work.

Like in the first round, time seemed to be passing impossibly fast. I kept glancing at the clock, wondering if it was moving faster than usual.

I sprinkled a little cayenne into the chocolate ganache for my chocolate cupcake, being careful not to add too much. I wanted the judges to feel the heat—not burn their taste buds off.

I added just a touch more and the whole lid came off of the container, dumping tablespoons of the bright red powder into my ganache. I bit back a yelp of horror as I grabbed a spoon and tried to dish as much of the cayenne out of the chocolate as fast as I could.

How could that have even happened? I'd been so careful not to add too much! There was no way I could have shaken the container hard enough that the lid would come flying off like that!

I looked up and saw the cooking assistant to my right—the D'jinn—staring straight at me.

Had she actually used her powers to make me use too much cayenne? I shook my head, even for me that was a little too far-fetched.

"This ganache is a bust," I told Iris as I went to scrape it out into the trashcan. "Check the cupboard. Is there any more cayenne?"

Iris came back, shaking her head. "I don't see any cayenne," she said with a frown. "What happened?"

I glanced towards the station next to ours. The D'jinn was still staring straight at me.

Iris followed my gaze with hers and gasped. "Did she... hex you?"

I shrugged. "I have no idea. It doesn't even matter if she did or didn't. I don't have time for this! I have to figure out a new solution for the ganache—and quick!"

"There's always chipotle," Iris suggested.

I nodded. The flavor of my favorite seasoning was much more pronounced than it would have been with cayenne—a little less heat, and an earthy smoky quality to it. "I guess it's going to be a snow-capped volcano," I joked.

Iris grinned as she went back to creating the decorations for the cupcake.

After that things kept going wrong—nothing big, and nothing I could really blame on the D'jinn girl, but enough to throw me off my stride.

"Crap!" I hissed as I knocked my jar of vanilla beans over, making it roll off of the counter. I grasped for it as it seemed to float inevitably in the air for one long, impossible moment. It slid right past my fingers and shattered on the floor.

I was so distracted by the pile of glass that I turned to snatch the cupcakes out of the oven just before they burned.

And I never burned things.

"And we're done in..." Owen Dark announced. "Ten..."

Iris rushed into throwing her beautiful decorations haphazardly onto my cupcakes. I grabbed her wrist right before she put the silver sparkles on the wrong cupcake.

She stared at me in horror.

"Eight..." Owen shouted.

The plate of cupcakes slipped in my fingers and only a quick grab by Iris kept them from sliding off and onto the floor.

"Three!"

I grabbed a rag and started cleaning off the plates while Iris put on the finishing touches.

"And we're done!" Owen practically screamed, jumping up and down. I noticed that not one of his perfectly moussed hairs budged, despite his energetic bouncing, "Bakers, stand away from your cupcakes!"

I glanced down at the cupcakes.

Despite everything that had gone wrong, they looked amazing. Iris really had done a Magical job at making the cupcakes beautiful.

All I had to worry about was the gelato filling melting before the judges got to it.

We lined up in front of the judging table.

I clasped my hands nervously in front of me. My palms were sweating so badly I thought they were going to start to drip onto the floor. Add in the shaking and I was about to become a one-woman sprinkler system.

I caught the eye of the D'jinn assistant back in the kitchen. She was still staring at me with that intense poker face. I couldn't understand why she would want to interfere with me and my baking. Cheating was so... shallow. I was here to see if I was the best baker and to challenge myself. How could I figure that out if everyone was willing to do just anything to win?

My attention dragged back towards the judges, where they were tasting the contributions from my competitors.

"Don't you think the coconut was a little... obvious of a choice for the theme?" Candy asked the woman next to me. "This round is about creativity. There's nothing creative about coconut as snow."

I swallowed. I had a coconut cake, too. Hopefully the lime in it would be original enough to earn points from the judges.

It seemed like an eternity before the judges got to my cupcakes. I kept picturing the pineapple gelato inside my mango cupcake melting away to nothing, making the whole inside of the cupcake turn to a soggy mess. Maybe

I had pushed myself too far, trying to create a cold cupcake during competition.

"Cindy," Owen said, with his wide smile, "why don't you tell us what you have for us here?"

I tried to smile back, but my face felt stiff. "Well," I said, swallowing the nervous knot in my throat, "You have here a chocolate snow-capped volcano with chocolate ganache and a fluffy Swiss meringue buttercream with real vanilla. The second cupcake is a snow-cold mango cupcake filled with pineapple gelato and topped with a dulce de leche frosting with just a touch of spice." I licked my lips. "The third cupcake I have for you is a coconut-lime cake topped with sparkling one-of-a-kind snowflakes on top."

"Well," Candy said seriously after tasting her plateful delicately, "I can see that you took the theme seriously and I appreciate that. The decorations are beautiful."

I shot Iris a hidden thumbs-up.

"I agree with Candy for the most part," Jeffries added, "the spice in the chocolate cake was smoky and really reminded me of a volcano. Unfortunately, I felt this cake didn't really fit the theme. It was too much of a stretch for me."

I nodded, feeling my smile flatten on my lips as I steeled myself for the comments to come from Kane.

Again, the guest judge had only taken a small nibble from each of my cupcakes. I wanted to shout at him that he couldn't get the whole experience of what I had created that way, but I resorted to twisting my fingers together instead.

"Interesting," he said flatly.

That was it. Interesting.

I had a feeling I was going home.

Chapter Nineteen

Iris gave me a squeeze as we were ushered into the scream-and-cry room to wait for the judges' decisions.

"I'm going home," I told her. "They loved your decorations, but I don't think they liked the cupcakes."

"Then they're crazy," Iris told me. "Those cupcakes were freakin' awesome. I don't see how anyone could have done any better." She whipped her head around to glare at the D'jinn sitting across the room.

I put a hand on her arm. "Don't make a big deal out of it," I told her. "It doesn't matter anyway."

"But they're cheating," Iris insisted loudly. "How can you let them get away with that?"

I shook my head at her, twisting the cap off of my water bottle and downing the contents in about three gulps. All this sweating was making me thirsty. "Let it rest, Iris. It's done and over with."

Iris crossed her arms over her chest, her face a study in fury underneath her rainbow hair. "Whatever."

The judges didn't deliberate for long. We filed out in front of them and stood patiently, waiting for the axe to fall.

I knew I was going to hear my name, so I almost walked out as the name passed Owen's lips.

"Libby Jenson," Owen announced, "I'm sorry, but this battle is over for you."

Wait, that wasn't my name!

I'd made it to the final round?

I had no time to wrap my head around the idea. Owen was already describing the event we were to cater for.

It was down to me and the baker with the D'jinn on her team. I could feel their eyes on me as Owen verbally danced through an uncanny number of witty puns to inform us that we were going to be making a display and cupcakes for...

"Ice Dancing with Stars!" Owen announced proudly.

Suddenly the snow theme from the last round made sense.

"Remember," Owen said charmingly. "In addition to the cupcake creations you made last round, we will expect to have three new flavors, all following our theme, all decorated and placed on a magical display that our construction teams will be assisting you with. In this round you will each have four baking assistants and three hours. The time starts... now!"

I didn't know if three hours felt incredibly long or impossibly short for the amount of work we had to get done. I was already wrung out and exhausted from the previous rounds of competition. How on earth was I going to be able to find the energy to create three new cupcakes and a display?

At least I had Iris by my side!

"The volcano cupcake isn't going to work for this theme," I told her, "We're going to have to come up with a different decoration for that cupcake."

She nodded. "Do you have any idea what you're going to do for the three new cakes?"

I shook my head. "I'm working on it. I was thinking of doing something with rose petals—you know how the skating performers always get roses after they dance?"

Iris nodded thoughtfully. "I can make the whole top of the cupcakes look like roses," she suggested.

"Make sure you have enough time," I warned her. "We have a lot of cupcakes to create."

I turned towards my new cooking team and grabbed a pen and a sheet of butcher paper. "Here are the recipes for the cupcakes we've already made. If you can get to work mixing these and getting them in the oven, that would be the most help."

The women nodded and set to work.

I breathed a sigh of relief. I'd just have to trust them to get the recipes right. It was nice to have some helping hands with the baking because I was going to have to focus on the new flavors.

I set to making my rose petal cupcake. I pulled all of the petals off of a bunch of roses and boiled them down into a quick jam that I could use for flavoring the cakes. There was a fine line, I knew, between rose petal flavor being sweet and elegant and it just tasting like... soap. I also intended to use the same jam in a mousse filling for the rose cupcake.

After that I had to turn my attention towards the two other cupcakes I still had to invent. I kept wracking by brain, but I had no inspiration—it was like beating my head against the marble countertops. I knew I needed to do something special and unique... This was my thing, so why was I pulling a complete blank?

I threw together the rose cupcake batter and headed towards the ovens to put them in to bake, still trying to think of something—anything—that I could come up with for the new cupcakes.

I slipped.

Down I went. Down went the cupcakes.

I sat in the middle of the floor, covered in batter and tried to ignore the fact that there was a camera trained on me.

Iris squeaked and abandoned her decoration creating to run to my side. "What happened?" she asked. "Are you OK?"

I tried to smile. "I think I broke my dignity," I said, "but other than that I am perfectly fine."

I groaned as I looked down at the mess all over me and the floor. I was going to have to start the rose petal cupcake all over again! At least I had made a ton of the jam, so I wouldn't have to start completely from scratch.

Well, I didn't have time to feel sorry for myself. I jumped up and got back to work—recreating the batter I had lost.

It was just happenstance that I looked up and noticed the D'jinn girl staring at me again.

Had she made me slip?

I couldn't be sure, but I was starting to feel more than a little unnerved by her always staring at me like that.

Didn't she ever blink?

"I'm going to make a sticky toffee pudding cupcake," I told Iris. "I'm going to make the sauce into the frosting—and I'm going to sprinkle candied bacon over the top. Can you work with that for decorations?"

She pursed her lips and nodded. "Yeah, I can work with that," she agreed. "I'll put sparkly ice skates on it with a swirl of chocolate to look like that pattern the ice gets—you'll see, it will be really pretty."

"I think I'll finish with a chocolate-chai cupcake with mousse inside and a chai cream frosting dipped in chocolate ganache," I whispered to her. "I know I can get that done in time. You'll just have to make decorations that will tie it in to the theme."

She nodded, her hands flying as she pieced together all the intricate pieces of edible art we were going to need.

After all, this was going to amount to two thousand cupcakes! It was crazy to even attempt half as many in this time.

I'd almost forgotten all about the display I was going to have to come up with when the team approached me, ready to take notes.

"I want lights," I told them, not even pausing in my baking to talk to them, "and sparkle, like ice, and... I want a spot light and a cutout of a gorgeous couple skating that spins around in the middle. I want the logo to be huge and on top of everything—light that up—and, can you put the cupcakes on rotating tiers? And... oh, I think the whole thing should be black, white, and silver."

They blinked at me.

"Um, we can try to get that all done," the carpenter said, rubbing his ear as he looked down at the list he had scribbled out, "If we start now."

"Then do it," I suggested. "Let's try to win this thing!"

Chapter Twenty

I didn't even raise my head again until the carpentry team was back with my display. I'd been working so hard and with such focus that it had felt like minutes, not hours.

Iris nudged me. "Look," she said, "the display—it's perfect!"

It really was. Somehow the team had managed to clean up my rather sketchy idea and make it into a beautiful, elegant piece of art. Black velvet and twinkle lights brought to life the turning of the ice-dancing cut out in the center and the multiple turning rings for the cupcakes that surrounded it.

"It's gorgeous!" I exclaimed, giving each of the men a well-earned kiss and grateful to see they didn't turn into toads. That would have been a disaster. "Thank you!"

After that it was all about finishing touches—that last dab of disco dust and the last fondant rose petal—and then packing all of those two thousand cupcakes onto the huge display.

Even with all of us—even the carpentry team—working together, it was right down to the buzzer. I tossed down the last cupcake and threw my hands in the air, not even caring that I was covered in icing and flour.

We were finally done! Win or lose, it was all out of my hands now.

It was time to face the judges for the last time.

Iris and I lined up next to the other baker—I'd never even learned her name—and her D'jinn assistant. I'd been so focused on myself all day that I realized that they were just as nervous as I was. The little blond baker was twisting her hands together and breathing through pursed lips in an effort to calm herself down.

This time it was my turn to present myself first. I swallowed down my nerves and plastered a grin onto my face. "I wanted to capture all the elegance and grace that is ice dancing," I told the judges. "For the three new flavors I've made for you a rose petal cupcake with rose infused mousse filling, a sticky toffee pudding and bacon cupcake, and a chocolate chai cupcake. I hope you enjoy them."

"Well," Candy said thoughtfully, putting her fork down and looking at me earnestly. "I can see you've put a lot of thought into your flavor profiles. This rose cupcake is unique and delicious. I'm going to have to steal the recipe."

I grinned.

Jeffries nodded. "I agree with Candy about the rose cupcake—it was delicious, but my favorite one would have to be the sticky toffee pudding one. It was really good."

Kane looked me in the eye and said, "Not bad."

"Annika," Owen said to my opponent, "why don't you present your display and cupcakes?"

Now that I was done with my part of the competition I was free to see what she had done. I was seriously impressed.

Her display was an actual rink with cupcakes decorated as skaters with tuxedos or sparkly gowns. Tiny spotlights lit the whole thing up from above where the logo was really prominent.

I couldn't remember what the judges had said about her cupcakes all day, but I did know one thing—there would be no shame at all in losing to a display like that!

"The three new cupcakes I have for you," she said in her rather breathy, soft voice, "are all themed around the kinds of skaters you see on the show. My first cupcake is a rich, nutty hazelnut pound cake with a fudge filling and chocolate Swiss meringue buttercream. My second cupcake is a delicate lemon cake with a bright Meyer lemon curd inside and topped with toasted meringue." She took a deep breath, "Lastly is my in-your-face cupcake. This is a raspberry cupcake with a raspberry mousse filling and a vanilla buttercream topped with raspberry popping candies."

I couldn't help but grin—I loved the way her mind worked. Those cupcakes sounded really good! I wouldn't have minded having my own plateful to try.

Too bad we were competing for the same prize!

The judges tasted each of the cupcakes carefully.

Kane grinned at her. "These cupcakes are absolutely spectacular!" he exclaimed. "I especially loved the lemon cupcake—lemon meringue pie is my absolute favorite dessert ever. These decorations are charming and appropriate. I love that they are all in costume and ready to skate. Well done!"

I tried not to stare at him. All competition he hadn't said more than a couple words to me about my cupcakes. Obviously, he preferred Annika's flavors over mine, but did he have to be so obvious about it?

"I enjoyed these cupcakes," Jeffries agreed. "Beautiful and delicious. Very well done."

"So charming," Candy murmured. "They're all dressed up and ready to go!"

Oh, well. It was pretty clear to me which direction the judges were going to go.

"Please step backstage while the judges deliberate," Owen said.

We went back to the little room and I grabbed another water bottle. I was tired, hungry, and really thirsty.

"When this is over," I told Iris, "we're going out and finding a really good place for burgers."

She nodded in agreement. "I'm starving," she said dramatically. She looked down at her fingers, which were dyed all kinds of colors from the fondant and glitter she'd been working with. They almost matched her hair. "I can't remember ever being so tired!"

"Amen," Annika interjected from across the room. "Ugh. I don't want to see another cupcake ever again." She paused, "Well, no more today anyway."

"I wouldn't mind eating some," I said wistfully as my stomach growled audibly. "Your cupcakes looked really good."

She smiled. "Oh, thank you! I think yours have looked great all day."

Iris made a grumpy noise. I tried to shush her, but it was too late. She frowned at the D'jinn girl sitting next to

Annika. "So, why were you trying to cheat?" she demanded bluntly.

I groaned to myself. "Iris!"

My sister crossed her arms over her chest. "No, I won't be quiet. All day we've been having trouble thanks to her."

The D'jinn put her hand on Annika's arm as the smaller girl opened her mouth to answer. When she spoke her voice was a soft, rich alto. "You're mistaken," she said gently. "I was not the one to hex your sister."

Iris sat back, astonishment all over her face. "You were not?"

The D'jinn shook her head. "I spent the whole day trying to keep your sister from getting into trouble. We D'jinn are sworn to protect her."

It was my turn to be shocked. "What?"

She nodded. "I know who you are, Cindy Eller. We are sworn to protect you from harm. I would never hex you."

"Why are you sworn to protect me?" I protested.

She shook her head. "I cannot speak of it, except that someone cares for you and worries about your safety."

I frowned.

Jessi. It had to be Jessi. After all, she was the only person I knew that had D'jinn connections.

"Then who cursed Cindy?" Iris demanded. "Who else would want her to look bad and lose the competition?"

The D'jinn girl shrugged. "That, I do not know. There are other Magical beings here today."

I nodded. Owen and Kane were both Magical. Either one of them would have been capable of hexing me.

But why would either of them want to?

Chapter Twenty-One

We filed back out in front of the judges for the verdict. All I could think about was the fact that the D'jinn were sworn to protect me and that I had been hexed for real. Without that protection, who knew what could have happened to me.

I was really grateful to Jessi for sticking her nose in my business.

"All today," Owen said to the camera, his dark eyes sparkling, "we have enjoyed cupcakes that were exquisite and unique. Both bakers have done a phenomenal job. Unfortunately there can only be one winner today. That winner is..."

I crushed Iris's hands in mine. I held my breath. It didn't seem possible that we could win, not when Annika's comments had been so much more complimentary than mine.

I couldn't stand the wait. Why was it taking him so long just to pick a name?

"Annika Pearson!" Owen shouted. "Congratulations! You are the winner of Battling Cupcakes!"

I let my breath out. Disappointment filled my gut, but at the same time I felt relieved. Now the whole experience was over with. I could get a burger, walk on the beach, and head home with my head held high.

And it actually had been pretty exhilarating.

"I have no regrets," I told the camera when it turned to me. "Annika really deserved to win. She did so well all day. I'm really happy for her."

I raised my eyebrows in astonishment as I saw Kane making his way towards me. He offered me his hand.

"I really thought you should have won," he told me brusquely. "Your cupcakes were far superior. I said so all day, but the other judges have no palates." He handed me a slip of paper. His card. "Call me. I'm very interested in taking your bakery..." his eyes flicked towards the camera, "Central."

I almost gasped. Central? As in Magic Central? That was a huge opportunity!

"Looks like you won after all," Iris said smugly.

"But," I protested, staring at him. "Then you weren't the one who..."

He shook his head and glanced over at Owen Dark. "Some people are... *Fairer* than others." he raised an eyebrow at me significantly.

"I'm sorry..." I started. "I don't understand..."

Iris nudged me. "Fair folk," she hissed in my ear. "Fairy. Owen Dark is Fae."

I swallowed. There was only one reason that a Fae would be on this side of the barrier... and out to get me.

And that reason was my father.

"I don't know why our fair young man would feel that way towards you," Kane said smoothly, "but try to be careful, yes?"

I nodded.

"You bet," Iris said fiercely. "Nobody messes with my sister."

Kane smiled at her approvingly. "Beautiful artwork, by the way. I know your father. He's absolutely brilliant. I do think that you may be a better artist than he is, though."

Iris glowed under his praise. Her cheeks nearly matched the stripe of pink in the rainbow of her hair. Her face flamed even further as he bent his head over her wrist and gave the back of her hand a kiss.

Looked like somebody was kindling a little spark for my sister.

If the expression on her face was any indication, the feeling was absolutely mutual.

I really missed Timothy. Looking at them—at that wonderful possibility in their eyes—I felt like a piece of me was missing.

Kane bowed to us both one last time and left.

Iris and I headed towards my car.

"So, we're not going to confront Owen Dark?" Iris asked. "He just gets away with it?"

I shrugged. "I don't know that he did get away with it. Thanks to the D'jinn, there was no real harm done."

Iris frowned. "That doesn't sound right, Cindy. He hexed you."

"We think." I shrugged. "Look, I'm on my alert now. What else is he going to do?"

Iris shook her head. "I don't know, but I don't have a good feeling about this."

I shook my head at her. "Is that a premonition?" I asked, "or is it just being worried?"

She frowned. "I don't know." She shivered a little, rubbing her arms. "Maybe a little of both?"

I put my arm around her waist and gave her a squeeze. "It's OK, Iris. It's a long story, but all I can tell you is that it involves my father. I don't know what Owen was trying to do—hurting me wouldn't hurt my dad at all."

Iris scowled. "Well, it would hurt me!"

We climbed into my car and I hand just started the engine when there was a tap on my window.

It was Owen Dark.

I really hesitated to open up my window when I was sure that he was the one behind my 'attack'. I wasn't sure why I did it, but after a moment I opened it and let him lean towards me.

"What do you want?" I asked. "You know, you can't get at my father through me. I don't even know him."

Owen Dark shook his head. "Whatever you think is going on out here is not as simple as you believe," he said seriously, all traces of his smarmy camera persona gone. I liked this Owen a lot better.

"Are you saying you didn't try to hex me?" I challenged.

Iris squeaked at my audacity.

"I did," Owen said bluntly, "but no serious harm would have come to you. I needed to keep you out of any more public attention. It's dangerous. I'm not the only one who knows who you are."

"That sounds... sinister," I commented.

He cracked a smile. "Good. It should. Be careful in the future. Don't take anything at... face value."

I frowned at him. "Don't any of you Fae folk talk plainly?"

He laughed, then sobered. "Your Magic," he said, "is very strong."

I nodded.

He gave me another enigmatic smile as he turned away.

He glanced back over his shoulder. "Say 'hi' to Sumac for me," he said as he disappeared into the shadows.

Chapter Twenty-Two

After such a long and exhausting day it was fun to just grab burgers and shakes and walk along the beach, talking to my sister. We'd grown up together, but I was realizing more and more that I hardly knew her as a person.

Sisterhood was so strangely intimate and not all at the same time.

"I love the ocean," Iris said dreamily, dragging a French fry through her shake and staring off towards the horizon. "I know you're not an Earth Witch, Cindy. Do you feel its... pulse? The way it breathes?"

I nodded.

"Art feels the same way, you know," she said conversationally. "Watch this."

She knelt down in the damp dirt—not the dry fluffy sand that made up most of the beach, but not the super damp stuff either—and used her finger to trace out a little figure in the sand. It looked a little like a pixie, but more ethereal, more airy... a sylph perhaps, clothed in her long wisps of floating hair. It was incredible—the detail my sister could create with one finger and the sand at her feet.

Then she dusted off her hands and breathed over the image.

At first I thought she was just blowing the extra sand from her picture, then the sylph moved.

And lifted off of the sand.

And flew away.

Leaving the blank sand before us.

"I'd forgotten," I said in awe, staring over the sea where the little sylph-figure had disappeared, "that your art really comes alive."

Iris shrugged, digging her toe into the sand. "It never lasts," she said softly. "They always fade away in the end."

We could have stayed another night in California, but we decided to head home instead. Iris took the first shift driving.

"Go ahead and sleep," she encouraged me. "I've got stuff going on in my head. I have plenty of company up here." She touched her forehead, a smile of self-mockery on her lips.

I yawned. "If you're sure."

She laughed. "Of course I'm sure."

"Just wake me at the half-way point," I told her. "I don't want you driving all night alone."

"Yes, Mama," she giggled, rolling her eyes.

I settled myself as comfortably as I could into the passenger seat and was asleep faster than I ever could have imagined.

I dreamed and I knew I was dreaming.

The trees grew around me—tall and proud—their branches kissed with a golden morning light. A strange, sweet-smelling perfume filled the air. It was such a heady scent that I couldn't help dragging in whole lungsful of the stuff. It smelled like the sweetest citrus blossoms every—but even sweeter.

I wandered through the trees—my bare feet cushioned in a thick layer of moss. The air was chilly—autumnal–but I didn't mind. I was warm enough.

I walked around one large tree trunk. It was the widest tree I had ever seen. I could have put my whole living room in there with room to spare.

I grinned. I quite liked the notion of living inside of a tree.

I ran my fingers against the rough bark as I circled it, stepping over the ridges of the roots under my feet.

I looked up and Timothy was standing there.

"Where are you?" I asked. I tried to reach for him, but my dream-self couldn't seem to do it. All I could do is look at him.

He looked at me sadly. "I'm lost," he whispered. He looked around the woods, turning his head in all directions.

"How do I find you?" I demanded.

He shook his head. "I'm lost," he repeated.

His form shivered and then disappeared.

I sat down in the shade of the tree. It was my fault that Timothy was lost and missing—because of me he wasn't leading the life he loved. It wasn't right.

Love should free someone, not take them away from everything that makes them happy.

I was bad for Timothy.

The realization hit me with a wave of visceral pain. I whimpered as I curled up on myself, tears streaming down my face.

A hand touched my shoulder.

"Have you seen my son?" asked Quinna Borden.

As the last time I had seen her, Quinna appeared to be about my own age and rather healthy and beautiful for a dead woman.

"He's lost," I moaned. "I don't know where he is."

Quinna just looked down at me seriously, a slight frown touching her forehead. "Have you seen my son?" she repeated.

Then, like Timothy, she vanished.

I climbed to my feet and screamed for Timothy.

I had to find him! I stumbled through the woods, searching for him. Maybe if I searched hard enough I would be able to find him and bring him home.

I awoke to myself shouting out Timothy's name.

Iris looked over at me from the driver's seat with a frown of concern on her face. "Are you OK?" she asked. "You were crying in your sleep."

I touched my face. It was wet. "Bad dream," I told Iris.

"Real dream or dream-dream?" she asked seriously, her eyes on the road.

I frowned. "Dream-dream, I think. I hope."

I stared out of the window—the dream as fresh in my mind as if I were still there. My heart still pounded in my chest from desperately trying to find Timothy among all those trees—hearing his sad voice telling me that he was lost.

And it was all my fault.

Maybe it was time to let Timothy go. Maybe if I did that, if I showed my father that I was willing to... move on... I swallowed. Even the thought of that made me feel a wave of despair.

But... maybe it would bring Timothy home.

Timothy didn't deserve this. He had been faced with nothing but trouble since our relationship began. First he had been turned into a toad, and then he'd had to deal with me being hounded by a prince... and now he had been kidnapped by my Magical father.

I crossed my arms over my chest, remembering every moment we had spent together. I could remember every single one—every flash of his dimple when he smiled—the way he brushed my hair off of my face with an almost reverent expression.

Timothy.

Oh, Timothy. How could I ever let him go?

But how could I ask him to go through all over this over and over again just because I was too selfish to let him go?

I pressed my hands against my face, trying to stem the flow of tears rolling down my face.

If I was so bad for Timothy, could I owe him anything less?

Chapter Twenty-Three

"I should have just had Iris drop me off at the bakery," I grumbled at the clock as I woke up only two hours after arriving at home.

All my dreams had been tortured and fragmented. I felt more exhausted than I had before going to sleep.

I showered and got dressed, my mind still in a miserable haze.

But I had made a decision. I would go to Magic Central and try to scry to my father to let him know that I was willing to let go—as long as he released Timothy from whatever prison he was being held in.

It was the right thing to do.

So why did it feel like my heart was broken?

I had never truly understood that phrase before. How could a heart feel broken? But it did. It hurt to breathe, to exist. I pressed my hands against my chest and let the tears roll down my face.

I tried to ignore the voice in my head that this wasn't fair.

So what if it wasn't? Life wasn't fair.

But I had to do the right thing.

I had to give Timothy his life back.

Hopefully my father would be willing to play fair.

"I hate you," I hissed under my breath at my unknown father who had stepped in and ruined my life. "I hate you!"

It didn't make me feel any better.

I pulled up in front of the bakery and climbed out, determined to follow through with my plan... and bury myself in a mountain of baking.

Hey, it had worked in the past. Maybe that was how to mend a broken heart—keeping myself too busy to think... or feel.

Hairy Guy still sat on the doorstep of the shop, wrapped up in his sleeping bag until only the tip of his furry nose stuck out into the chilly morning air.

I smiled to myself as I opened the shop and pulled together a breakfast for the two of us. I remembered how much he liked milk, so I brought out a half-gallon and two glasses.

"Hi," I said softly, as I brought my tray outside and sat down next to Hairy Guy. "I hope Jessi treated you well while I was in California."

I handed him a cinnamon roll and bit into one myself. It wasn't one of mine, but it was still pretty good. My little sisters were becoming excellent bakers.

Hairy Guy pulled his cinnamon roll apart, eating in quick, hungry little bites. I poured him a glass of milk.

"I'm glad to see you," I told him. "Even if you don't recognize me or care or anything. It's nice to have a familiar face when you are sad. I'm sad today."

I didn't know why, but it felt so easy just to tell Hairy Guy everything that I'd experienced in California—everything except the real reason why I was sad.

I set my chin in my hands. "And I know it doesn't mean anything to you—that I miss Timothy. You never met him, but he's a really great guy. Anyway, it's my fault that he's missing and isn't getting to live the life he wants. It's not right." I sniffed. I didn't want to cry anymore. I had had enough tears.

Hairy Guy reached over and patted my hand.

I looked over at him, shocked. He still didn't even look at me, but he left his hand over mine.

It was surprisingly comforting. I gave his hand a squeeze. "Thanks for listening to me," I told him. "It's always nice to have a friend."

I could have sat there all morning, but I had chores to do. I gave Hairy Guy's hand another squeeze.

"If you need anything," I told him, "please come into the bakery. You know you're always welcome."

He didn't answer, but for the first time I thought he understood.

It was nice to bake in my own territory with no deadlines or competition hanging over my head. I patted my pink mixer—the one Tansy had bought when we opened the shop. Using it always made me think of her.

More than the house I lived in, this place was home. It was where I felt the most together—where I created and where I was able to express myself.

On a day like today, when I was in emotional turmoil, it was nice to be able to return to my center and just be me.

I set to rolling out dough for my batch of morning croissants. Adding the butter layers took all my attention and was a great distraction.

I knew what the right thing to do was, but I didn't want to do it. I had to let my father win this round so Timothy could get his life back.

So why did it feel like I was giving up too easily?

Starrie and Rainey arrived at the bakery full of their usual energy and abounding with questions about my trip to California.

"I'm not allowed to tell you!" I reminded them.

"But... did you win?" Starrie insisted. "Come on! You can't just leave us hanging like this!"

I smiled. "I'm not telling. You'll just have to wait until it airs on TV."

Rainey pouted. "Which will be like in a hundred years," she protested. "We're your sisters. Can't you let it slip to you?"

I laughed. "If I told you then the whole universe would know. You two can't keep a secret to save your lives."

"That's what you think," they chorused together in a rather foreboding manner.

I hated to think what kinds of secrets the two of them kept.

Starrie poked at my rising pumpkin-roll dough and peeked into the oven to check the cookies that were baking in there— cranberry with macadamia nuts and white chocolate chips and pumpkin oatmeal were the cookies of the day.

"How did things go while I was gone?" I asked them. "Was it more work than you were expecting?"

Rainey shrugged. "Yes and no. Nothing we couldn't handle."

"Yeah," Starrie agreed. "We only had one fire while you were gone—no biggie."

I cringed. "A fire?" I tried not to shout the words, but they still came out a little too strongly. "What happened?"

"Oh," Starrie said easily, flipping her hair over her shoulder and displaying the ornate butterfly tattoo on the side of her neck, "I was trying my hand at frying doughnuts and the oil got too hot."

Rainey nodded. "It was so not a big deal," she agreed. "It's not like we don't know how to use a fire extinguisher."

I glanced around my little shop, wondering if I had missed the signs of such a huge occurrence. Everything look perfect and pristine to me.

"As if we would tell you if there had been trouble," Starrie said, a glint in her moon-silver eyes.

"Seriously," Rainey echoed.

They looped pinky fingers and grinned cheekily at me. "We can keep secrets."

Touché.

Chapter Twenty-Four

I was just pulling a batch of pumpkin-date pies out of the oven when my mother came into the shop.

I waved at her and carefully slid the tarts onto a rack to cool before going to greet her.

She kissed my cheek as she looked around the shop, her eyes taking in the innocent way my sisters were working—Iris decorating a birthday cake while Starrie messed with a cupcake recipe and Rainey helped Jessi at the register, handing out samples of our new cookies. Knowing my mother, she didn't miss a thing.

"What brings you here?" I asked her, returning her kiss. "You know I'll send you anything you need."

My mother smiled. "Do you mind if I just hang around today? I've been wanting to really get to know this venture of yours a lot better, since everyone in the family insists on working here."

I frowned to myself. My mother had never been a real fan of my baking. In a family of over-achievers, I had always felt like I was an outcast—especially since my Magic had never been as powerful as that of my family.

Recently, though, my mother had announced that all of those beliefs of mine were false—I actually had very powerful Magic, which she had stifled to try to protect me from my father.

I still couldn't wrap my brain around the idea. I was completely unaccustomed to using my Magic. I didn't even know what I was capable of. It was easier just to slide into letting my Magic work its own way through my baking and not try anything fancy.

Whether it was habit or fear that I would still fail, I really didn't know.

"Of course you're welcome here," I told her. "I'm about to make a bunch of apple-cardamom tarts. Do you want to help?"

She nodded. The sparkle in her eye made her look far too young to be my mother, not to mention a mother of six... soon to be seven. Magic was kind to the aging process.

"I always did like baking," she admitted. "Not that I would have ever made a career of it."

"How are you feeling?" I asked her, as we settled down together to chop and season my apple tart filling.

She pursed her lips. "The nausea comes and goes," she admitted. "Cindy... I *am* sorry that I didn't tell you right away. I was kind of in shock..."

"It's OK," I interrupted her. "And... I'm very excited to have another sister... or, I suppose it could be a brother. Are you going to find out this time?"

She smiled, shaking her head gently. "No. It's one of the most Magical parts of having a baby—that beautiful mystery. Plus... well, I've only had girls up to this point, so I figure this will be another one."

"Marcellus," I said thoughtfully, thinking of my stepfather's name. "I can't think of a single fairytale twist you can put on that name."

"I'll think of something," she answered, popping a piece of apple into her mouth.

Poor kid. I wouldn't put it past my mother to have Stephan change his name so that she could work her evil way on this unsuspecting baby's name.

All was fair in love and motherhood, I supposed.

I sighed. Not that I would ever know.

I hadn't really given much thought to having kids. I didn't even know if I wanted any. Until recently every guy I had ever kissed had immediately turned toady... with warts and all.

Timothy had been my first glimmer of life and love beyond toad-hood.

And now I was losing him too.

"What's wrong?" my mother asked, putting her hand over mine. "Don't tell me it's nothing. I can see it in your face."

I hesitated as I looked up at her. Mom had never taken my relationship with Timothy seriously. For one thing, he was an Ordinary and my mother did not consider any Ordinary to be good enough for one of her children.

But she looked so loving and... motherly at the moment that I found myself blurting the whole story out to her—about Sumac and Timothy missing, about the warning at the contest... about my decision to let Timothy go.

To her credit, Mom just listened. She didn't interrupt my story or interject her own opinion. She just frowned thoughtfully as I finished, running her fingers across the countertop.

When it was clear I was finished talking she tucked her hands together and regarded me seriously. "I do believe that your father means well," she said slowly. She held up her hand as I opened my mouth to protest, "Even if he is doing it in the most idiotic and heavy-handedly misguided way imaginable."

Well, I agreed with her about that!

"Am I doing the right thing?" I asked softly. "It hurts to even consider letting Timothy go—but I don't know any other way for him to be free of my father's interference. Whatever he's being put through—he doesn't deserve it."

My mother pressed her fingers against her lips—a sure sign that she was thinking about this seriously. "What does your heart say?"

"I don't know!" I wailed, then lowered my voice as I caught the eye of the customers staring at me. My mother shook her head at me. She didn't approve of losing one's composure.

"I don't know," I repeated, more quietly. "I want what's best for him... but the thought of letting him go..." I sucked in an agonizing breath. "It's the hardest thing I've ever had to do."

My mother looked down at her hands. "Then don't," she said.

"What?" I asked, confused. "Don't?"

Mom looked up and me with her dark, serious eyes. "Don't let him go," she said firmly. "Listen to your heart. If I had... oh, all those many years ago, you wouldn't be going through any of this. Do I think he's good enough for you? Of course I don't. No man is ever going to be good enough for one of my girls." She reached out to brush a curl of my hair back away from my face. "But, if you love him," she said, "if your heart is all tied up in him... don't let your father, me, or anyone else stand in your way. If your love is true it will work out. I honestly believe this."

I tried not to stare at her. These words from a woman who had been married twelve times—from the woman who seemed completely driven by her success and fame as the most powerful Earth Witch of her generation.

Somehow it was all the more moving, coming from her.

"If I had done things right," my mother said, her eyes focused off in some distant land I couldn't see, "you would have known your father and he would have known you. He would have been able to teach you about your Magic and abilities and your... heritage. It's my fault that you don't have any of that. I do hope that my mistakes won't completely, irrevocably ruin your life."

I cringed. I had accused her of just that, once. I reached over to give her a hug. "You have only ever tried to protect me," I told her. "That's what mother's do. And I'm glad that you are mine."

"And mine!" Iris sang from her corner.

"And mine!" Starrie and Rainey echoed.

My mother grinned, tears sparkling in her eyes. "Oh, I do love my girls," she laughed, opening her arms to all of us.

"Good thing," Starrie quipped, "since you keep having more of us."

"Yep," Rainey agreed. "The more the merrier, right Mom?"

My mother regarded them with a narrow expression, biting down on her lips. "Maybe," she said thoughtfully, "this time I'll have a boy."

Chapter Twenty-Five

It was a good thing that my mother's unexpected pep talk had set me back solidly into my resolve of keeping Timothy, for my father was not even close to easing up on me.

In the week that followed I had no less than five separate encounters with various Magical creatures—each one that insisted that I immediately become his bride and go off with him.

"Really?" I shouted in exasperation as I shut the bakery door behind the last one—there had been three today alone. "A centaur? What was my father thinking?"

While centaurs were definitely great for riding off into the sunset with, I just wasn't interested in dating one.

Jessi stifled her giggle behind her hands. Alecto didn't even bother trying to hide his mirth. He laughed openly at me, leaning over the counter as his peals of laughter filled the bakery.

"Nice," I growled. "Nice of you to appreciate my humiliation... yet again!"

Jessi coughed back another laugh, then collapsed against Alecto, guffawing in earnest now. "I thought the toads were bad," she gasped, "but a centaur? Whoo! Your father must have kind of sense of humor!"

"Or something," I agreed. "I'm inclined to think he's a heavy-handed jerk, but then again... he's my dad!" I faked a goofy grin. "Lucky me!"

"I want a centaur," Starrie said wistfully, looking after the specimen in question with longing in her silver eyes. "We could go for long rides on the beach..."

"Yeah," Rainey agreed, faking a swoon, "it would be so romantic!"

I narrowed my eyes at them. I couldn't tell if they were in earnest or poking fun at me. Knowing them, either was a distinct possibility.

And Hamish had been handsome in his own way—with hair a couple shades orange-er than my curls on his head and a strapping bay Shire horse-portion. If only the two halves were separated he would have been enough to make any girl swoon.

That and his rather thick accent.

I wished him luck in finding a suitable filly to woo.

Listen to me, I was getting all old-fashioned and Magical with my vocabulary! 'Woo' indeed!

"I'm going to take Hairy Guy a snack," I informed the room at large. "When I come back I hope you will all have the decency to be through with laughing at my expense."

I shook my head, trying hard not to grin as I traipsed out the door. What had my father been thinking? Surely the centaur was a joke!

Right?

"This has gone way too far," I told Hairy Guy, handing him a glass of milk and a sandwich to go with the stack of cupcakes I'd been sneaking him all day. "I don't suppose you have an ideas about getting my father to stop this parade of male specimens into my life and getting my real boyfriend back?"

Of course, Hairy Guy said nothing. At this point I figured that was a good thing—he would probably just poke fun at me with all the others.

"My father," I told Hairy, "is driving me crazy. I keep telling myself that his intentions are good, but it's getting harder and harder. What was he thinking—sending a centaur here? At least he was a wearing a really good illusion spell." I shook my head. I could have gotten into some serious trouble with the Council of Magic if Ordinaries had spotted a centaur coming out of my bakery.

Hairy Guy finished his sandwich and reached out to give my hand a squeeze. He had become much more comfortable with touch the last few days. I scooted to sit closer to him. I found his presence to be soothing anytime I was agitated—as I was now.

Well, pretty soon I would be launching my first bakery stand in Magic Central, thanks to Kane following through with his offer to help me get launched. Hopefully my father would hear about it through whatever grapevine he was entangled with and start sending Magical dates there instead of into the open where just any Ordinary could see them.

My phone buzzed in my pocket and I flipped it open to answer it. "Yes?"

"Cindy," a voice said quickly, "it's Sumac. Don't say anything out loud. Can you meet me at the portal—just order a ton of tacos and wait for me there? I need to talk to you right away."

"Of course," I said quickly. "Is it... about Timothy?"

"I can't talk," Sumac answered. "I'll be there as soon as I can."

I put my cellphone back into my pocket, wondering at the urgency in Sue's voice. She wasn't even supposed to be on this side of Faerie—something was wrong.

I swallowed hard.

I really hoped it didn't involve Timothy.

Tacos Y Margaritas was a little hole-in-the-wall wannabe Mexican pub, but they made some of the best tilapia tacos I had ever had in my life. They even had a spicy mayonnaise that made me consider rethinking all my opinions about the nastiness of mayo in general.

"Fried or grilled?" the bored waitress asked as she dropped a bowl of greasy tortilla chips and another of salsa onto the table in front of me and frowned when I requested my three orders of fish tacos fried.

It was worth every bit of her judgmental scowl when I bit through the piping-hot crisp covering on the subtly sweet fish with the cabbage and spicy mayo slaw on top.

I hoped Sumac would hurry up or I was going to have to order another whole batch of tacos. The waitress was really going to stare at me if I did that.

I was just biting into my second taco when Sumac arrived from the bathroom—looking like she was trying out for a role in a bad spy movie.

She pushed back her huge sunglasses to blink at me with her startlingly blue eyes. "I'm glad you could make it," she said quickly, snatching a taco and pouring half of our serving of salsa on top of it before biting into it with a sigh. "Gods, there is no good Mexican food in Faerie. The La Llorna folk aren't cheerful and nobody asks a chupacabra to dinner."

I didn't know if it was appropriate to giggle or not. "What's going on?" I asked her. "Is it Timothy? Is he OK? Is he hurt? Did my father do something to him?"

Sue held up her hand to stem the tide of my verbal onslaught. "Hold on a second," she mumbled through a spray of crumbs. "Ma mowf is fuh."

I tapped my fingers restlessly on the surface of the table as she chewed—how many times did she have to chew each bite anyway?

"Two things," she said quickly, picking up another taco and staring at it. "First off—there's some kind of issue with your Magic."

I blinked at her. "There is?"

She nodded. "I don't have any details, just that your dad and my mom have been arguing about it a lot... and that's never a good thing."

I sat back. "You have no clue what they're arguing about?"

She shook her head.

"The other thing has to do with Timothy," she said softly, looking up into my eyes with her huge blue ones.

I leaned forward. "What?"

"He's missing."

Chapter Twenty-Six

"What do you mean he's missing?" I asked. "I mean, of course he's missing—I wouldn't be sitting here every day waiting to hear from him if he wasn't missing!"

Sumac shook her head. "No, no," she said, "you're not understanding me. Your father doesn't even know where Timothy is anymore... wherever he had him before... well, he's gone now. I don't know how long he's been gone, but apparently it's been a while. I just found out about it."

I stared down at my plate of tacos. Suddenly my appetite was gone. "My father doesn't even know where he is?" I echoed, my voice sounding strangely odd even to my own ears. I looked up at Sumac. "He doesn't even know how long Timothy has been gone? What happened?"

She shook her head. "He must have escaped," she said. "Lenus has been practically tearing Faerie apart, searching for him."

I frowned. "Lenus?"

She nodded. "Your father."

It took me a moment to take it in. My father had a name. No one had ever told me his name.

It made him seem more... real.

I stared at Sumac with the realization that she had stood face-to-face with my father and talked to him—

and I never had. I had a million questions for her—I desperately wanted to know what he was like, but all those would have to wait.

"Where would Timothy have gone?" I asked.

Sumac shook her head. "I was hoping that you would be able to tell me that. Can you think of anything that would have driven him to run away? Lenus... Lenus said that Timothy wasn't... all there." She winced at the outraged expression on my face. "He imprisoned Timothy in his own mind," she said apologetically. "At best... Timothy would be a shadow of his usual self. He has no memories... nothing. He's a clean slate."

"I have to find him!" I shrieked. I reached across the table and grabbed Sumac's arm. "You have to take me to Faerie! I'll be able to find Timothy—I just have to!"

She shook my hand away. "You can't," she said. "Anyway, I told you—Lenus has already gone through Faerie with a fine-toothed comb. Timothy isn't there anymore. He has to be somewhere in the Ordinary world."

"No," I breathed, trying to imagine what it would be like to be Timothy—wandering around without his usual wit or skills. What if he got hurt? What if someone took advantage of his state and hurt him?

I knew that Sumac was still talking to me, but none of her words made any sense to me. All I could think about was the fact that Timothy was out there somewhere—robbed of his wits, robbed of his life—and it was all my... no.

It wasn't my fault. It was *his* fault.

My father's.

Rage welled up in my mouth. "You can tell my father," I ground out from between my teeth, "that he has gone way too far. He wants to mess with my life? Well, he doesn't know what he has gotten himself into."

Underneath my hands the table was starting to shake. I was so furious that I couldn't see anything—a sheet of red hot rage covered my eyes.

"Cindy!" Sumac's voice came from a distance. "Cindy, calm down!"

I couldn't calm down. I was livid. My fingertips dug into the table. It felt like the entire room was shaking around me.

"Cindy," Sumac said soothingly, "breathe. You can't do this here. You have to calm down! This isn't going to help Timothy!"

I sucked in a deep breath of the frigid air-conditioned air and tried to steady myself. Deep down I knew that Sumac was right—none of this was going to assist Timothy—wherever he was.

The room slowly began to clear in my vision. I shook my head, shaking the last tendrils of red from my eyes.

Sumac reached out to touch me and yanked her hand back, hissing. She shook her fingers out as if she had burnt them.

I dropped my head, still gulping in lungs full of oxygen. I stared down at my hands. The table all around my fingers was singed and crumbling.

"What just happened?" I asked Sumac.

She shook her head and licked her lips. "I think it's safe to say that you're starting to come into your powers. You getting upset just now must have triggered them."

I just stared at her. "My powers?" I croaked. "What kind of powers are these?"

She twisted her lips in a crooked smile. "Well," she said, "seeing as you are a half-breed... we have no idea what you'll be capable of."

"Oh, great," I groaned. "I guess this is what you came all the way from Faerie to warn me about?"

She nodded even as she hushed me.

I wasn't supposed to talk about Faerie out loud.

I yanked my hands away from the table and looked down at the new, deep scars that I had created.

"Is this sort of thing going to happen often?" I croaked. "I can't exactly go around burning things up. I'm a baker."

Sumac shook her head, her thick curls bobbing around her delicate face. It was hard to remember that she was over a hundred years old when she looked so... adorable.

"I don't think any of us knows what to expect," she admitted. "After all—your mother is a powerful Earth Witch... and your father..."

"Is basically a god," I said.

Sumac waved her arms to shush me again.

"I really don't think anybody is sitting here and listening to us while they eat their tacos," I muttered.

"You never know," Sumac said darkly.

"Oh, that reminds me," I said. "Someone wanted me to say 'hi' to you."

Sumac blinked at me. "Who?" she asked.

"Owen Dark."

Sumac turned gray and slumped into her chair.

"Owen Dark," she said flatly.

I nodded.

"Oh, crap," she whispered. "This is so not good."

Chapter Twenty-Six

I had never seen Sumac look so deflated. She sat for a long moment, just staring down at the floor, her face an unflattering shade of gray under its usual golden tan.

"What is it about Owen Dark that makes you turn... puce?" I asked.

She glanced up at me and rubbed her head. "I don't even want to know what you've been up to if you ran into Owen Dark," she said.

"What?" I said, shocked by the suspicious look she was giving me. "I was on a cupcake baking competition. He was the host. You know—grinning at the camera and making bad puns? Sure, he tried to hex me, but Jessi's D'jinn connections took care of that..."

Sumac brightened visibly. "The D'jinn are following through, then?" she said. "Oh, good!"

I narrowed my eyes at her. "So, am I to take that to mean that it was you and not Jessi who asked them to keep an eye on me?"

She nodded. "I've been worried," she admitted. "Your father has some people that aren't very happy with him."

"Gee," I muttered. "I wonder why."

Sumac flashed me a brief smile. "Anyone with that much power is going to make enemies," she said with a shrug. "Believe it or not—your father is one of the good guys."

I made a face. "Tell that to somebody whose life he hasn't screwed with."

Sumac shook her head. "Yeah, I know that one." She looked up and grinned at my expression of surprise. "What? You think I'm immune just because I'm his niece? Believe me, that is not the case at all! And I've been around longer than you to get messed around with!"

I kind of felt sorry for Sumac for a moment. After all, my father had only been messing with my life for a few months—not a hundred years!

"So," I said. "What is the deal with Owen Dark? I mean, I get that he doesn't like my father—I don't really like him at the moment myself, you know—but why does that make you turn gray?"

"Owen Dark," Sumac said distastefully, "is *evil* . His whole clan is. They are manipulative and... well, you don't want to be mixed up with them."

"Still sounds like my father to me," I quipped.

Sue shook her head seriously. "Cindy, trust me. Owen Dark is way over your head. He has absolutely no compunction... he will do anything, absolutely anything to get his way."

I frowned. "Still sounds like my dad," I muttered.

"Look," Sumac said desperately. "Owen Dark was kicked out of Faerie for starting an uprising in which he completely wiped out three clans of the Sidhe—the High Ones. They were his friends, Cindy. He smiled at them, he ate at their tables, and then he killed them with his own hands as they slept. I can assure you that your father is nothing like Owen Dark." She spat out the name.

I stared at her.

Goosebumps rose along my neck as I realized how badly I had misjudged this man. I hadn't taken him seriously because of his endless posturing in front of the camera—his toothy grins.

Even when he had hexed me I hadn't taken me seriously.

Iris had.

I owed her a huge apology.

"Well, it's not like he's here now, right?" I asked. "He's all the way back in California. He tried to hex me and he failed. All is well, right?"

Sumac hesitated before she shook her head. "I wish I could believe that," she said seriously, "but Owen Dark is notorious for holding a grudge. He would kill you just to avenge himself on your father."

I frowned. "My father? What did my father do to him?"

Sumac sighed. "He's the one that captured Dark and cast him out of Faerie," she said. "Owen Dark swore he would get revenge on him and destroy his family." She looked up at me, her piercing blue eyes staring straight into mine. "I think you should be worried."

I swallowed. "He was playing with me," I muttered, "at the contest—smiling at me, looking all innocent. Pretending to be my friend... all along he was planning on how to kill me?" My voice squeaked on the last words.

"Very likely," Sumac admitted. "Well, you know better now. It's a good thing I came here and was able to warn you. You need to be on your guard."

I nodded. "Thanks, Sue," I said softly.

She smiled. "Anything for my cousin, right? With parents like ours, we have to stick together."

For the first time I realized how little I knew about Sumac's life. One of these days—when things has settled down and Timothy was back where he belonged, I was going to make a point of getting to know her a lot better.

"Oh, and Cindy," she said as she stood up, grabbing a last taco to take with her back through the portal. "Be careful with your powers. Work with that stepfather of yours, OK? You really don't want to lose control. It would be disastrous."

I grimaced as I nodded, looking down at the full hand prints burned into the table in front of me. I didn't think I would ever forget that.

"I'll be careful," I promised as I gave Sumac a hug. "You're not going to get in trouble for being here, are you?"

She flashed a grin at me—back to her usual perky self. "Only if I get caught," she whispered with a wink.

I laughed as I watched her go.

At least I had one ally on my father's side of the family.

I had the feeling I was going to need all the help I could get.

But first I had to find Timothy. He was out there somewhere, lost and alone, and I was complicit in his situation, even if it hadn't been my fault directly. I needed to find him— and I was going to.

Instead of heading towards the door, I headed towards the bathroom—and not because the tacos had been bad. I was going to go through the portal to Magic Central.

I needed to find my stepfather.

I was going to try to scry for Timothy again.

Chapter Twenty-Seven

My stepfather wasn't at his club, which meant he had probably actually gone home for once. I crossed the main street on Magic Central and headed for the closest portal to the home where he lived with my mother and the twins.

They lived in a cozy cottage on a small, private island in the Puget sound. My mother had created a portal in the woods a short walk from their front door—just another sign of how much clout she had in the Magical community.

It had been way too long since I had visited. The flowers along the walk were new to me—as were the two rather fat cats who greeted me just outside the door. Warm lights glowed invitingly from the windows. All in all it looked cozy and comforting.

I felt like an intruder.

It was the first time in my adult life that I realized that my mother was her own person—this was her private life—and I shouldn't have just appeared without warning at her front door.

But it was too late for such thoughts. The front door was already swinging open and my mother stared at me in surprise. "Cindy!" she exclaimed. "What are you doing here?"

I should have brought some treats. I felt lame standing there with nothing to offer her. "I have a problem," I said. "I need your help."

Mom stepped back to let me in.

"I'm sorry I didn't call ahead," I said, taking in what had obviously been a quiet evening for two—the twins were nowhere in sight and my stepfather sat in front of the fireplace with yet another cat on his lap and a teacup on his knee.

Mom shook her head. "You don't have to call," she said in a matter-of-fact voice. "This is your home, even if you never lived here."

I took a deep breath. "I need to scry for Timothy again," I said. "Something's wrong... S—someone has informed me that my father has lost Timothy. He's no longer in Faerie. No one knows where he is." I swallowed, blinking back tears. "I'm terrified that something must have happened to him. It would be all my fault..."

My mother took my hand and guided me to the couch. She gave me a gentle shove until my knees bent and I sat down.

"First off," she said briskly. "None of this is your fault, as we've discussed. Secondly... certainly we can guide you through scrying for Timothy. Thirdly... when was the last time you ate something that wasn't completely based on sugar?"

I blinked at her. "I had some fish tacos," I reassured her.

She sighed and rolled her eyes, but didn't comment on my idea of a healthy meal.

"As it happens," Stephan said, putting down his saucer and stroking the tiny cat that was perched on his knee, "we have a scrying bowl here at the house." He stood up and handed me the kitten as he crossed the room to get his materials together.

Of course they did.

"Thank you," I said quietly as I watched the pair of them work together to help me with my problem.

"Nonsense," Mom said, frowning as she whisked the kitten away from me and disappeared into the other room—returning shortly with an ewer of water.

This time, instead of staring into the water and searching for answers myself, I was surprised when my mother reached across and took my hands. She nodded towards Stephan and he took my other hand, until we stood over the water in a ring.

I had never been strong enough with my powers to work with other people. As I felt the energy cycle through the three of us I wondered how much I had missed in my earlier years, not being able to take place in the Magical community this way.

I could feel their power joining to mine and settling together. Mom's Magic was earthy and sweet-smelling with a scent of pine needles and fresh basil teasing my taste buds. Her hands were dry and soft in my grasp, reassuring and calm.

Stephan's Magical touch was efficient and disciplined. At first I couldn't really make out his affinity, then I realized that he, like my mother, was an earth power... but his power was redolent of cool, damp places—caves and caverns full of mystery and minerals.

His Magic had a deep foundation. It felt steady and cool against my jumble of unknown Magic.

My mother inhaled deeply. Stephan and I matched our breathing to hers as we looked into the still water inside the big black bowl.

"Timothy," my mother whispered, reminding us of our focus.

Timothy. It was easy to focus my mind on him. I had been thinking about him nonstop lately. What was harder was removing all my fears and worries about him from my thoughts. I had to focus on him—the feel of him in my life—and allow that feeling to show me where to find him.

The water was dark for a long moment. I could feel the power build up around the three of us, all focused on finding the man I loved and bringing him safely home. The electricity in the air reminded me of monsoon season in Tucson—when lightning could lace across the sky with no warning.

The surface of the water flickered with lights. Images flew past faster than I could see clearly. I thought I could make out Timothy holding my hand as we stood on 'A' Mountain back at home. Then another flash of him as a tiny toad, sitting on my shoulder. I thought I saw him walking through a marketplace in a foreign land, that curious, bright glint in his eyes that I loved so much.

I leaned forward as the water brightened. Surely, next I would see where he was now! Excitement raced through my veins.

The surface of the water burst into a flurry of bubbles. My mother cried out as Stephan yanked us away from the bowl.

The scry boiled and hissed into a cloud of steam.

When I blinked my eyes to clear them the image was gone.

And so was the water.

The bowl was completely dry.

"Well," Stephan said thoughtfully, "that's a new one."

Chapter Twenty-Eight

Mom and Stephan stared at me.

They'd been staring long enough that I was starting to feel a little uncomfortable.

"So," I said lamely, "I guess the water isn't supposed to evaporate like that, huh?"

My mother chewed on her lower lip, but didn't even blink.

"Um," I said, "you guys are really starting to freak me out—staring at me like that."

My mother blinked and sighed, shaking her head as if to clear it.

She glanced at my stepfather. "I've never even heard of that happening," she said, "have you?"

Stephan shook his head. "I don't even know what would make it possible," he admitted.

They both turned their heads to stare at me again.

I sighed. "Was it me?" I asked, "or was it my dad?"

"Oh," my mother said positively, "that was all you."

Stephan nodded. "I could feel your Magic charge right through me." He rubbed his arms reflexively, remembering the sensation. He shook his head. "I've never felt anything like it. It's... not fire Magic precisely."

Mom nodded. She grabbed a cookie from the plate on the coffee table and nibbled on it. I thought she looked a little green.

I hoped she wouldn't throw up.

"It's almost Fae Magic," she said seriously, "but that's not quite it." She looked up at me. "I would say that it is all your own."

I bit my lip. "And this isn't the only time my own special Magic has messed up today," I admitted. I flopped down onto the couch beside her and described my meeting with Sumac.

As I talked I could see two pairs of eyebrows rise higher and higher.

Stephan shook his head as I finished. "I don't like this," he said, rubbing his upper lip in his familiar gesture. "I've never seen Magic like this. I don't even know how to begin helping you get it under control."

My mother hesitated before nodding. "It is both like and unlike your father's Magic," she said. "I don't know how to help you, either."

I frowned. "Do you know who could help me?"

I had a feeling I wasn't going to like the answer.

I was right.

Mom and Stephan exchanged a long look. He got up from his seat. "As a member of the Council of Magic," he said, "I believe it would be wise if I weren't party to the rest of this conversation."

He left the room, trailed by three cats.

I shook my head. My mother had really let go of her opinion that witches should never own cats.

I looked at her and knew what she was going to say before she even opened her mouth.

"You have to go train with your father," she said seriously.

I winced. "I can't do that! For one thing—it's illegal for anyone to cross the border in and out of Faerie—even if it seems like everybody and my mother are doing it."

She winced.

"Secondly—I don't even know my father! The little I do know about him does exactly instill me with the desire to go straight up to him and say, 'Hey, Pops! nice to meet you. Can you help me fix my screwed up Magic?'"

Mom shook her head. "Cindy," she said with a note of exasperation in her voice. "He's the only person I know that knows anything about your type of Magic."

"Well, what if he can't help me either?" I asked. "Not that I'm willing to go to Faerie and hunt down a man—who I am furious with, by the way!—to train me illegally in my forbidden Magic, but what if I did? What if he couldn't help me either?"

Mom shook her head. "I don't know," she admitted. "I'll be blunt with you, Cindy. You have strength and abilities that concern me. It doesn't feel quite like fire Magic, which you know is dangerous, but it doesn't feel safe, either. I'm... very worried that you could get hurt by your powers. I don't want to put you through what I experienced when I was seventeen. There is a reason why our worlds are closed to each other. I know that now and I believe that it is wise—but I am your mother! I would rather have you break a thousand laws and be safe than risk you being burnt out or worse because we don't know how to handle your powers."

"Can't you just bind them again?" I asked meekly.

She shook her head wryly. "No," she admitted. "You're far too strong now for me to even attempt it."

That admission set me back more than any other experience the whole evening. My mother was the most powerful Earth Witch of her generation—possibly even the most powerful witch altogether.

If she couldn't bind my powers, chances were that nobody could.

I rubbed my eyes. I was starting to get a horrible headache. "It's just all this worry," I told her. "I'm sure all of this would go away if I just knew where Timothy is. I start worrying and then my Magic gets out of control. I just need to find him." I looked up at her. "Maybe you and Stephan could scry for him without me?"

My mother shook her head. "I'm sorry, pet, but I never met him. You know that the stronger the emotional attachment the more likely it is that he would be found. There would be basically no point in me even trying."

I sighed. "I figured as much."

The drain on my powers and all the emotions hit me all at once. I felt too tired to even lift my head.

"Do you mind if I crash here tonight?" I asked. The cushions on the couch next to me were starting to look very inviting.

"You're always welcome here," my mother said simply, digging into the chest next to the couch and coming up with one of her hand-woven blankets. She tucked it around me. "This is your home."

Chapter Twenty-Nine

I awoke with a cat sitting on my forehead and no clue where I was.

"Did you hear her snoring?" I heard a giggle.

"I think that was the cat," came an answering voice.

It all came back to me in a flood. I sat up at glared at the twins, who were sitting next to the couch watching me like a pair of owls perched on the arms of Stephan's chair.

Starrie tittered. "Your hair is standing straight up!"

I reached up my hands to smooth down my rambunctious curls. "Don't you have anything better to do than watch me sleep?" I demanded crossly.

"Looks like somebody woke up on the wrong side of the couch," Rainey quipped.

"As if that's even possible," I said, rubbing my eyes and stretching. Each of the girls, I noticed, was holding a kitten.

"How many cats do you guys have, anyway?" I demanded. "What happened to Mom's 'witches don't own cats' rule that we had when I still lived at home?"

"Ten," Starrie said.

"Twelve," Rainey corrected.

They looked at each other and shrugged.

"It's always changing," Rainey said. "They keep showing up at our door."

"And it's not like we're going to turn them away," Starrie said practically.

"And then Snowdrop had kittens," Rainey added.

"Fourteen?" they chorused together.

"Do you want another cat?" Rainey offered. "Snowdrop's kittens are old enough to go off on their own now."

"Yeah," Starrie agreed, "and Mom wants to find most of them new homes before the baby gets here."

I pursed my lips. I wasn't in the right frame of mind to bring a new kitten home, even if I was sure that my own cat would be OK with it.

"Let me check with Merlin first," I said tiredly. "I'm sure Jessi and Iris would be ecstatic... as long as you warn the kittens about the dangers of hunting Iris's pets." Though I wouldn't really miss the parrot that much. He took way too much enjoyment in making fun of me doing yoga.

Maybe I could convince Merlin that he needed a few less tail feathers.

"We'll ask Merlin," Rainey offered.

"I'm sure he won't mind," Starrie agreed.

I couldn't help but grin. "OK," I agreed. "I just don't want to end up with as many animals as Goldie, OK? Last I heard she had a baby dragon at her house."

"I know," the twins said wistfully.

I shook my head. "How about I get cleaned up and you give me a 'ride' to the bakery?"

The girls nodded and bounced off with way too much energy, considering I was pretty sure it was still dark outside.

We barely beat Jessi to the bakery. She frowned when she saw me. "I was so worried!" she said, shaking her head until her wild curls bounced. "Where were you all night?"

"Sorry," I said. "I had a kind of emergency and I went home to talk to my mom and Stephan. Next thing I knew I was sleeping over."

"Well, call next time!" Jessi gave me a little shake. "I almost had kittens, I was so worried."

I yawned. "Talk to those two about kittens," I told her, tilting my head towards the twins as I set to unlocking the front door and getting my day started.

"Good morning," I told Hairy Guy as I handed him his breakfast. He would have to do with day-old cinnamon rolls and milk until I got something warm out of the oven.

He really didn't seem to mind at all.

"He's the best-fed bum on the block," Jessi said cheerfully as I passed her to get back to work. "No wonder he stays here day and night."

I shrugged. "I like having him here," I admitted. "I don't know why, but it feels like he's keeping an eye out for us."

Jessi grinned. "You know, it's funny that you say that, because I've been thinking the same thing! I asked Alecto about it and he said we should never take for granted a friend in any hour—whatever that means."

I frowned. It had just crossed my mind that perhaps Hairy Guy was one of the guardians Sumac had set up for me—even if the twins claimed they had found him wandering around. Why hadn't I thought to ask her about him?

Well, it made sense, especially when I took into consideration the golden Magic twisting all the way around him. It did look a bit like the Magic I had seen around Sumac while she was working at the bakery.

"Guardian angel?" I murmured to myself. "I never knew they were so furry."

I caught Starrie and Rainey staring at me again as I started whipping up a batch of pumpkin chai macarons.

"What is it?" I asked as I caught their eyes for the third time in as many minutes. "Have I sprouted a third eye?"

The girls shook their heads in unison.

"Mom told us about last night," Starrie admitted.

"We're supposed to keep an eye on your Magic," Rainey added. "Did you know that it's all... glittery and has, like... sparks in it?"

"Embers," Starrie corrected. "It looks so weird."

I frowned. Of course I couldn't see my own Magic. It was like trying to see the back of my own eyes. "My Magic looks weird? I mean, has it always looked weird, or is this something new?"

Starrie and Rainey exchanged a long look and shrugged.

"I don't remember it looking this weird," Starrie offered.

Great. Now my Magic even looked different.

I'd never tried to fit in, but it would be nice to have one part of my life be normal for once.

I was distracted from my morose thoughts by the appearance of a line of pigeons dancing the Can-Can on the roof over the shop door.

Luckily it was early enough in the morning that most people missed it.

"What were you thinking?" I hissed at the twins as I tried unsuccessfully to shoo the pigeons away.

They just kept on dancing, though a few of them peeled away from the group to dance a rather dramatic Argentine Tango.

They even had tiny roses in their beaks.

My sisters were nothing if not thorough.

"We were bored," Starrie complained. "Nothing exciting ever happens here."

"It's not like it's a big deal," Rainy added. She giggled. "The pigeons are enjoying themselves."

"I don't need to get busted by the Council again!" I hissed. "Stop this right now or I'm calling Mom!"

"No fun," Rainey pouted.

"Spoilsport," Starrie added.

They glanced up at the roof and the birds immediately stopped dancing. They shook their heads and coo-ed as if wondering what they had just been doing.

"Why?" I demanded. "You were being so good!"

Starrie shrugged. "We had to be good to keep our jobs," she said.

"Yeah, but now we're indispensable," Rainey agreed. "You're not going to get rid of us."

"Just try me," I muttered.

The twins just grinned at me.

"Hey," Starrie said. "Do you think if we get Cindy really mad she'll start a fire?"

Rainey looked hopeful.

"Great," I muttered. "You had to get back to normal now? You couldn't have had worse timing."

"We know," the girls chorused.

Chapter Thirty

Despite my growing belief that my sisters were hoping that I was going to burn something down—the bigger and the more dramatic the better—I didn't have a single issue with my powers all day.

There were no more disturbances with the pigeons, either.

But, of course I spent the entire day waiting for something to go wrong. I figured my desserts were just a little more... precise as a result.

"There's never enough chocolate in a day," Iris sighed as she popped one of my famous miso-caramel truffles into her mouth. "I could eat chocolate all day every day and never get sick of it."

"If you work here long that's exactly what you'll be doing," I told her.

Jessi and Alecto were taking the shift with the food truck, which meant Iris had spent the day in the kitchen with me and the twins. I figure she, at least, didn't know about my Magical mishaps yesterday, because she wasn't treating me any differently than usual.

I watched as she absently drew a dove in the flour on the counter with her finger. She blew over it gently and the bird peeled off of the counter, flitting around the shop a few times before it turned back to dust.

"That never gets old," I told her, shaking my head. "That is a seriously cool talent."

Iris grinned. "It's fun," she admitted. "I can keep myself entertained with it."

I tried to imagine what it would be like to be able to create moving, breathing art like that. I shook my head. I couldn't even comprehend what it would be like.

I'd probably create a whole menagerie at once and cause a panic in the streets of Tucson.

I could see the headlines now.

"I don't suppose," I said wistfully, "that one of your little critters would be able to find Timothy for me?"

Iris made a soothing sound and put her arm around my shoulders. "I'm sorry he's missing, honey," she said. "I could try... you know, they last a little longer if I use paint or something."

I blinked the tears out of my eyes. "You would do that for me?"

She squeezed me again. "Of course I would! You'd do the same for me in a heartbeat!"

"What kind of materials would you need?" I asked, sniffing back a sudden onslaught of tears at her kindness.

She pulled at the strings of her apron. "There's an art store on the corner," she said. "I can get everything I need and be back in a flash. I can't promise that it will help, but I will try!"

"Thank you," I told her, sniffing again. "You have no idea what this means to me."

She squeezed my hand. "Sure I do," she said. "Hope is a wonderful thing. You've given it to me. All I can do now is try to return the favor."

I really had the best sisters in the whole world.

How did only children manage?

Iris was back within twenty minutes and hummed to herself as she set up an easel in the back of the bakery and started dabbing at her canvas with what I assumed were oil paints. I didn't know how artists worked in general, but it seemed to me that she was painting at an extremely fast pace. In no time at all, it seemed, she had numerous tiny and intricately detailed creates dancing across her canvas.

"We need the detail," she explained to me. "The more attention I put into the art, the longer they last... and the more intelligent they seem to be." Her hand hovered over one image with an almost maternal air.

She really loved what she did, I realized. This kind of art was where her heart was—and where her Magic truly shone.

She never would have been happy working as an architect in another person's firm—not when her art could live and breathe.

She blew over the images on the canvas.

It took longer this time before the creatures snapped off of the page and gained dimension. They were pretty little thing—some were airy and bright little sylphs, creatures of the air. Other were short and squat and reminded me of a cross between a garden gnome and a guinea pig, with truly huge eyes and long eyelashes.

They danced around their creator as they came to life, twisting and turning and giggling with glee. They were like tiny little children.

One of the sylphs lighted on my shoulder and sat there, regarding all this new world with huge, bright eyes. It was impossible to believe that this was just a temporary creature.

How could Iris ever let them go when their Magic had passed?

"Close your eyes and picture Timothy," Iris told me. "Try to share your emotions with them. They will understand emotions better than words. It's hard to explain, but focus on how Timothy *felt* when he was with you."

I closed my eyes and thought about Timothy. I thought about the pressure of his hand on mine. I remembered the way his dimple would hover in his cheek as he teased me. I imagined the way he looked when he talked about a new ice cream flavor he had dreamt up, or the way he would tuck a curl of my hair behind my ear as if it were of the utmost importance to him.

I remembered the way he made me feel—love just didn't seem like enough of a word to express it. He made me feel whole and complete just being myself. He made me feel anchored, like all was right with the world in general.

He made me believe that life was beautiful and adventures were worth seeking. Risks were worth taking when he was there.

"Good," Iris whispered.

I snapped back to the present. I was clutching the counter so tightly with my fingers that my knuckles had turned white.

At least nothing had burst into flame.

The little creatures were swirling around me now. I could catch the scent of paint on the air as they danced faster and faster.

Suddenly they vanished.

"If he can be found they will find him," Iris reassured me, squeezing my arm.

I blinked back tears.

"Thank you," I whispered.

Chapter Thirty-One

Most of the little critters may have been doing their job, but I found a couple of them sitting with Hairy Guy later that evening, sharing a coffee cake with him.

Even paint-and-Magic creatures liked my baking.

I found another one soaking in my tub when I got home from the bakery, up to its furry little neck in cinnamon-roll scented bubbles.

I had to admit a good bath sometimes felt a little bit like being in love. I'd have to forgive the mistake, even if it was taking up my tub and using up my bubbles.

I found Merlin curled up on my pillow with a rather reproachful expression on his face. Apparently I was in for another guilt trip.

"Yeah, yeah, I should have called," I told him. "Sorry. I guess I'm just not used to someone waiting up for me. Will you forgive me?"

He regarded me through slitted mismatched eyes, but his purr echoed through the room, so I figured we were good.

"I could have used your help last night, too," I told my cat, flopping down beside him on the bed and wondering if I could recover part of my pillow for my own use. "Oh, and I think I'm supposed to ask you if you want a little brother or sister... of the kitten kind."

I opened my eyes long enough to ascertain that Merlin was staring at me. I couldn't tell if his expression was shock, curiosity, or animosity.

Heck, he was a cat. It could easily be all three.

"It's up to you," I told him. "I'll even let you pick out which kitty we bring home. That sounds kind of creepy, doesn't it?"

I couldn't tell what he was thinking, but he did move enough for me to cram part of my face up onto my pillow.

I was too grateful to press the point.

I needed some serious sleep.

"Rise-y, shine-y! Time for Yoga!" squawked the most annoying voice on the planet right in my ear. "Good morning to you, good morning to you! It's time to get up now! It's time to go p–"

"Merlin," I muttered into my pillow. "You so have my permission to eat that freakin' parrot."

"Ooo," the parrot returned, "I so scared. Big bad kitty. Bu Hao!"

I rolled over and glared at the brilliantly colored bird with as much animosity as my sleep-deprived brain could muster. "I do not," I said slowly, "have to argue with a brainless feather-pated avian first thing in the morning. This is my house. Do you pay rent?"

The parrot ruffled his feathers. "Cindy mean," he said in a little-boy voice, sounding pitiful and sad.

Oh, no. I was not going to let the stupid bird make me feel guilty now. "Yes," I agreed, "Cindy is very mean. Cindy thinks parrot stew sounds great for breakfast.

Cindy suggests that parrots don't come into her room ever again."

The parrot made a rude sound and flew away, muttering under its breath.

"Does Iris know you know words like that?" I called after him. "She's going to wash your beak out with a cleaning spell!"

I wondered if Iris could paint his beak closed.

Well, the damage was done. I was up for the day whether I wanted to be or not.

I fought the urge to put my pillow over my head and try to go back to sleep.

On the bright side, I actually had time for breakfast before yoga. If I got lucky, maybe I could even skip the latter.

"Any news?" I asked Iris as I shuffled past her to see if we had any non-sweetened cereal in the cabinet for breakfast. I ate far too many sweets to want sugar on my bran flakes. "Did any of your critters report in?"

She shook her head, her rainbow-colored ponytail bouncing on the back of her neck. "It's too soon to tell," she said. "After all—they have to find Timothy first and then make it back to report. That is—if they even manage to find him at all. We probably won't see them until this evening at the earliest."

I decided she didn't need to know about the one in my bathtub last night. I didn't want to get the poor little thing in trouble.

"I don't know how I'm ever going to wait that long," I admitted. I rubbed my hands over my eyes. All night my dreams had been strange and fragmented. Even now I felt a little off balance. "By the way, if that parrot of yours comes into my room ever again I'm making soup out of him."

Iris chuckled. As usual she had Chloe, her miniature bat, clinging to the top of her ear like a cuff. She lifted one finger to run it down the little creature's suede back. "Sorry about that. Matthias is overly enthusiastic about exercise. I think his last owner let him watch too much Richard Simmons."

That explained a lot.

"Hey, boss," Iris said, around a mouthful of yogurt, "can I get off work a little early today?"

I shrugged. "Sure. Why not? What's up?"

She turned a little pink, which looked interesting against the rainbow stripes in her hair. "I have a date."

"Oo," I teased, "Nice. Anyone I know?" I looked closer at her and she avoided my eyes. "Wait a minute! Is it *Kane* that you are going out with?"

She blushed further.

"I knew it!" I crowed. "I knew you two liked each other. That is so *cute* !" There was something truly adorable about the idea of the staid and serious business man Kane going out with my artistic be-rainbowed little sister.

Iris made a face at me. "So, I can get off early, then? I want to have enough time to get ready. He's taking me ballroom dancing."

I whistled. "Nice. Classy and romantic," I commented. "Sure, of course I'll let you off—take as much time as you need."

Iris grinned. "Thanks, Cindy."

I shrugged it off. "I just think it's neat that you are dating a big shot in the Magical community. Mom's going to flip her lid... in a good way."

Iris frowned. "About that..."

I mimed zipping my lips shut. "She won't learn it from me," I promised. "I don't know how long you'll be able to keep it a secret, though. Mom has eyes and ears all over. She's bound to find out sooner or later."

"Hopefully later," Iris said with a sigh. "Do you have any idea how many guys she's managed to chase off over the years?"

I shook my head. "I didn't really have that problem," I said. "I was more caught up in worrying that my date would turn into a toad. Mom didn't even have a chance to chase anyone off. I was perfectly capable of doing that on my own."

Iris giggled.

"If I let you off of work early do we still have to do yoga this morning?" I asked wistfully.

"Absolutely," Iris said. "It's good for you. Don't be such a pansy. Suck it up."

"Great," I grumbled. "And I thought your parrot was bad."

Chapter Thirty-Two

I rubbed my head as I peeked into the oven to check on my triple-chocolate chipotle brownies. All day I'd been fighting off a headache. It wasn't anything horrible, but it was distracting when I was trying to plan Amy's baby shower, which just had to be the baby-shower of the century.

Amy's wedding had been such a big deal that I had no idea how to even start trying to outshine it. I knew we had to plan everything around the twins theme—something that would have been a lot easier if I knew if they were expecting two boys, two girls, or one of each.

At least it wasn't triplets. I didn't even want to think about making three full-sized thirteen-layer cakes for the party.

"I don't know why you're stressing about it," Jessi said, walking by with a fresh load of treats for the dessert truck. "You have months to plan it."

I frowned at her. "It has to be absolutely perfect," I said. "Amy is one of our best clients. Where she buys, all her werewolf friends follow." I didn't even need to add that all of Amy's werewolf friends were stinking rich.

Someday I needed to find out how werewolves made that kind of money.

Jessi nodded. "That's true enough." She leaned over my shoulder to look at the somewhat-sloppy sketches I had been working on. "Are you seriously going to try to make the tiers of the cake move?"

I nodded. "I got the idea at Battling Cupcakes," I told her. "I was thinking it would look a little like one of the mobile things that babies have over their cribs. What do you think?"

Jessi shook her head. "If you can pull it off it would be awesome. What flavors are you thinking of using?"

I frowned in thought. I loved using chocolate in as many of my desserts as I could, but that didn't work for the werewolf crowd—a good number of them were allergic to chocolate. They were kind of like dogs in that way, not that I would ever say such a thing out loud.

"I want to figure out how I can use all the flavors from my pork rinds in a way that still says 'decadent' and 'sweet'," I told Jessi. "I just haven't figured out how to do it yet."

Jessi shook her head. "All this just reminds me why I am glad that you are the baker and I'm just in charge of the money and the marketing. Pork rind cake just doesn't make sense to my brain."

I grinned at her. "Yeah, well, webpages and rows of numbers make me go cross-eyed. I think it's a good thing we work together, or the whole business would go up in flames."

Jessi winced at my choice of words. "Hopefully not flames," she murmured.

Alecto came up behind her with a stack of cupcake boxes. "Ready to get going?" he asked. "I just twitted to let everyone know we'll be at the park in fifteen minutes."

Jessi nodded. "Sure thing. I just need to grab that last box of truffles and we can get going."

"You know," I said, as Alecto left through the front door, whistling cheerfully, "I may have misjudged him. I thought he was up to no good when I first met him."

"Oh, he is," Jessi said cheerfully, "but I've got him under control."

I shook my head at her. I didn't know how to react when she talked about her boyfriend like that.

It wasn't exactly reassuring.

I just had to trust that Jessi knew how much she could handle. She wouldn't thank me if I interfered in her personal life.

Not that I ever would. I knew how it felt to have someone meddle.

After they left I took advantage of a momentary lull in customers to take Hairy Guy a snack. I sat down next to him on the door step. It had become part of my daily pattern to take a moment to just hang out with him.

There was something quite soothing about sitting with someone and not even needing to talk. I knew deep down that I didn't really know anything about Hairy Guy—where he came from and why he was here.

I'd have to remember to ask Sumac about him the next time I saw her. I was pretty sure she had sent him to be my guardian.

I just really wanted to know what he was guarding me from.

I felt like I was walking through a mine-field blind-folded. I didn't know enough about my father's world and his friends and enemies to be prepared.

Sumac obviously believed that I was in enough danger to ask the D'jinn and Hairy Guy to watch over me. Who knew who else was out there trying to protect me from things I was too ignorant to worry about?

A couple of Iris's little paint creatures were still hanging around with Hairy Guy. They'd figured out pretty quickly where all the treats came from. As I watched he broke apart a cactus-fruit and plum muffin to share with the little critters.

I rubbed my head. As the day progressed my headache was getting worse and worse. Now it felt like a dull ringing behind my eyes.

Hairy Guy saw the gesture and reached out to squeeze my hand.

I shook my head. It was probably nothing more than needing a little more sleep and protein and a little less sugar. Anyone who lived on as many treats as I did deserved to get an occasional headache.

Not to mention the yoga hell Iris had put me through this morning.

People were not supposed to do that with their hips. I didn't care who you were, it just wasn't natural.

And that was coming from a witch.

"I bet no one ever bullies you into doing yoga," I told Hairy Guy. "I don't understand why people say they love it. It's nothing more than masochism at its finest."

I could have sworn that a smile touched his lips under all that fur.

"Don't tell me that you're like a cat," I moaned. "I bet yoga is easy for you, isn't it? You should see Iris. She practically turns herself inside out and seems to enjoy every single moment of it. She's sick, I tell you." I chuckled to myself. "Sick and *twisted* , right?"

I sighed as I stood up and dusted my pants off. "Well," I told him, "I'd better get to work. I'm on my own today. The twins bailed on me—something about proctored exams—and Iris is getting ready for a date. It sure seems strange and quiet without them around."

"Well, that's convenient for me," said a voice out of the shadows.

I whirled around to face Owen Dark. He leaned against the wall with a nonchalant air, a smirk on his handsome face.

I wondered how long he had been standing there, listening to me talk to myself.

The little creatures at Hairy Guy's feet hissed and disappeared into midair.

Yeah, that worried me a little.

Chapter Thirty-Three

I glanced towards the front door of the bakery, wondering if I would be able to bolt inside and lock it—and whether that would do me any good—before Owen Dark could make a move.

It was doubtful.

"To what do I owe this pleasure?" I asked, hoping that the sarcasm wouldn't drip through my voice.

"It really isn't this easy, is it?" Owen said, crossing his arms across his chest theatrically and looking me up and down. " 'Master' Lenus's daughter, completely unprotected?"

I tried not to glance down at Hairy Guy. I didn't feel unprotected with him there at my feet, even if Owen was dismissing him completely.

I was desperately grateful not be alone right now. That tingly spidey-sense was running all up my arms and back, warning me that something was seriously wrong.

"Lenus's daughter?" I repeated. "I'm sorry. I don't know my father at all."

Owen snorted. "As if I would believe that with his Magic practically covering you. You might be able to pass that off to someone who doesn't have the Old Blood, but I know the Old Magic when I see it. It's practically oozing out of your pores."

"Are you sure it's not just my own Magic that you are seeing?" I actually was wondering that myself.

Owen shook his head at me as if I were a particularly pathetic specimen. "You? A half-blood? Hardly! Do you think that kind of Magic just appears anywhere? If that were the case I would be *Rhee* , not that hot-headed idiot father of yours. That kind of power doesn't breed true."

"I honestly don't know my father at all," I told him. "I've never met him and I am far from being his greatest fan."

Owen rolled his eyes. "Nice try, pet, but I don't believe you." He walked towards me.

I tried to step back and found I couldn't move at all. I tried to drag in a deep breath, but all I could manage was to squeak in the tiniest amount of oxygen.

"Well, well, well," Owen said, circling me and eyeing me up and down in a manner that made my skin crawl over my bones. "You're a bit of a Magical mess aren't you? How can anyone make any sense of this? There's a reason why half-breeds are frowned down on. One false move and you'd burn this whole block down."

I swallowed, or tried to. I couldn't seem to move even that much. My mouth was painfully dry. My breath rasped through my lips as I strained to move. A wall of panic welled up inside of me.

I was trapped inside my own body.

I'd never felt more powerless.

Hairy Guy didn't even move. Maybe, like me, he couldn't. I could almost feel him still sitting at my feet, looking up at us with wide eyes.

Owen ran a finger down my cheek and rested his palm over my heart. "Well," he said with that side-ways grin that had made him a television sweetheart, "why don't we give you a little nudge, eh? That will send my message to Daddy bright and clear... with an emphasis, my dear, on 'bright'. Let's wake the sleeping dragon, shall we?"

He closed his hand into a fist over my chest.

Wrenching pain flickered along my spine. I screamed in agony.

I felt my Magic slip out of my control.

The world around me flickered with flames.

Owen Dark laughed as he disappeared in a swirl of purple-black sparks.

He really had a thing for theatrics.

With him gone, I gasped in a huge breath of air. I had to get the pain under control. I had to grasp hold of my Magic and force in back down inside of me.

The ground trembled beneath me. The air tangled with curls of heat and flame licking against each other. I could feel my skin tighten and crisp around me, cracking into fissures of red-hot agony.

Jessi chose that moment to come back. I could sense her on the periphery of my mind—racing towards me with a scream on her lips.

"No!" I shrieked. "Don't come near me!"

Flame poured out of my mouth, burning all the way down through my core.

I saw Alecto grab hold of Jessi as she screamed, reaching towards me. He dragged her back.

Good. At least she would be safe.

I tried to gulp air into my burning lungs, but it just seemed to fan the flames higher and higher. I tried to remember how to move, how to grasp hold of my Magic, but it slipped through my fingers.

The flames leapt higher and higher, taking me with them.

I had no choice but to succumb, to let go of all understanding of self, and let myself become one with the flame. To burn.

To burn until I was gone.

Strong hands grasped my arms. The air filled with the stench of singed hair. A chest pressed against my own—it felt icy cold against my flames. A deep voice cried out in guttural agony.

Hairy Guy.

"No," I gasped.

His howls of pain filled my ears, but he would not let go, even when I tried to throw him away from me. He had to let me go! He would burn up, too!

I struggled in his arms, but his grip never wavered for a minute.

"Cindy," he whispered as if to remind me who I was. His voice came from a long way's off. I could barely hear him.

"Cindy," he repeated, a little stronger.

His tears hissed against the inferno of my skin.

"Cindy, Cindy, Cindy," he chanted, holding me tighter and tighter and fur singed and skin burned.

His voice echoed through me.

Yes. Yes, I knew that name.

Somewhere in the flames his voice found me.

I was Cindy. I wasn't born of flame. I was of flesh and bone and blood.

My inner fingers grasped hold of my Magic, twisting it together, binding it to me. I grasped it with both my hands, spinning it down and taming it.

Cooling it.

I was not fire. I was not flame.

I was Cindy.

I gasped back to myself, the red receding from my eyes, the pain leaving my broken skin as it flickered and healed.

I held a charred body in my arms, whimpering in desperate agony.

"Cindy." It was Hairy Guy. I could scarcely recognize him in the features in front of me, they were so distorted underneath the charred hair and blackened, cracked skin.

He had called me back from the brink. It was he who had saved me from myself and my Magic. I had heard his voice when I couldn't even remember my own.

And yet—it wasn't him at all.

I knew him for who he really was.

"Timothy," I breathed.

Chapter Thirty-Four

The halls of the Healer Hospital were sterile and uninviting, yet I found their very blandness a reassuring contrast to the chaos inside of my head.

How could I have not known? How could I have missed that Hairy Guy—this stranger that I felt so comfortable with—was actually the love of my life, my Timothy?

My Timothy who was currently in a Magical burn unit in critical condition.

Because he had saved me.

I sat next to his side, not even daring to hold his hand because he was burned so badly there wasn't a single part of his body that didn't hurt at the slightest touch.

What made it worse was that he was completely alert and aware.

"Cindy," he whispered through cracked lips.

I winced. "Don't try to talk," I hushed him.

"I found you," he whispered in answer.

I felt tears prick my eyes. "Yes, you did," I told him. "You found me."

"I couldn't remember," he said breathlessly. "All I knew was I wanted to be near you. I didn't know... didn't even know who I was. When I touched you... I almost knew. I knew you were home. When... he hurt you... I knew. I knew you."

A tear rolled down my cheek and splashed down onto the back of his hand. He didn't even wince or pull away, though it must have hurt.

"I love you," he whispered, closing his eyes tiredly.

"I love you, too," I whispered back, wishing I dared lay a hand against his face, somehow show him what I was feeling.

I didn't dare cause him even more pain.

The tears were falling in earnest now. I couldn't hold them back any longer. Every second of worry I had felt about his disappearance. Every terrifying moment with my Magic taking over, every moment translated into the torrent of painful tears that rolled down my cheeks.

"I'm so sorry," I whispered, bending my face over his hand, weeping as silently as I could so as not to disturb him from his uneasy rest. "So, so, very sorry. I love you so much... and love shouldn't hurt this much."

I let the tears slide down my face. They had a will of their own, these tears of mine. They felt like they were pouring straight out of my heart and through my eyes. Every drop seemed to ease the intolerable pain I had been carrying with me for so long—all the fear and worry about Timothy, about my father, everything...

The headache that always burned behind my eyes started to ease as the tears wiped it all away.

I felt like they were cleaning out my very soul.

"Cindy."

I looked up at Timothy's whisper.

And stared into his face.

His beautiful, whole face.

"What?" I whispered. "How?"

Timothy's hands reached for me and I whimpered as I went to him. I climbed onto the narrow healer's cot next to him and curled up against his side, burrowing in as if I would never ever have to leave again.

"Your tears," Timothy said, his voice full of awe. "I have never seen anything like it, Cindy. Your tears healed me!"

I stared at his face, at every inch of him, unable to believe the change. He had been so damaged—so close to death's door—and now here he was, whole and beautiful again.

Timothy laced his fingers through mine—his beautiful, whole hand pressing palm-to-palm against mine. For the first time I understood Shakespeare's line about palms touching being a kiss. I had never experienced a gesture more romantic, more Magical.

And I was a witch.

"I love you, Cindy," Timothy murmured in my ear, his lips brushing against my cheek and along the corner of my cheekbones to linger softly on my lips.

"I love you," I murmured back, clinging to him.

He was here, he was whole, we were finally together.

I tucked my head into his shoulder as he slid into a deep sleep.

I had so many questions to ask him. How had he found me? How had he escaped from Faerie? Why hadn't he told me who he was? Had he even known?

The answers would have to wait.

My mother appeared in the doorway, her arms full of flowers. Sunflowers, I noticed, for healing, and white roses for true love.

She had really hit that nail on the head, I thought.

How else could I explain any of this? Timothy and I were supposed to be together. Our love was something special. Surely the miracle I had just witnessed had proven that.

Mom set the flowers down on the little table next to the bed and stood looking down at me.

"You really do love him, don't you?" she said, tucking my errant hair behind my ear and gazing seriously into my eyes.

I nodded, a lump in my throat making speech impossible.

She shook her head to herself as she settled into the chair I had vacated.

"How?" I managed to ask her, gesturing towards Timothy's healed, whole, face—the face I had feared was damaged beyond repair.

Mom shook her head. "We really know nothing about your kind of Magic," she admitted. "There is still so much to learn."

I shivered as I remembered the way my Magic had roared through me, uncontrolled. It had nearly destroyed me and Timothy—and who knew what else would have been torched in the conflagration.

"I wish you could bind it," I told my mother, curling more tightly around Timothy, as if I could protect the pair of us from myself. "I don't want Magic like that. It terrifies me."

"Rightly so," my mother said honestly, if not reassuringly. "I can't bind it, dear one. You're going to have to learn how to control it, one way or another."

I knew what she was going to say.

"You need to contact your father," she said sadly, looking down at her hands. "I know of no one else who can keep you safe."

I sighed. "I will," I promised. "Not today, but soon."

I knew, even as I agreed to it, that soon would always be too soon for me.

Chapter Thirty-Five

"Try this," Timothy said, holding one hand over my eyes while the other pressed an icy-cold spoon to my lips.

I obediently opened my mouth and let him feed me the creamy contents.

"What was that?" I asked, licking my lips, and trying to identify the flavor. It was familiar—but not at the same time. I couldn't quite place it.

"Pomegranate olive-oil gelato," Timothy announced, grinning down at me with the boyish grin that always made my heart flutter in my chest. "What do you think?"

I licked my lips again. "I think I need a larger sample," I suggested, trying to snatch the blank white container from his hands.

He laughed as he held it high over my head, a teasing expression touching his lips. "No way, my love! This is a special flavor for the party tonight!"

I groaned as I sat back down next to the counter. All day I had been trying to forget about the premiere of my TV debut—my episode of Battling Cupcakes was going to be on tonight and I was not looking forward to it.

All my friends and family had, of course, decided that it was the perfect opportunity to have a huge party, with me catering, of course.

I had spent the day making tiny bite-sized treats of all kinds, trying not to think about how embarrassing it was going to be to see myself on the TV like that.

If I ever found out who had come up with the idea of making a premiere party I was going to make them pay.

My money was on Jessi. She was just way too smug about the whole thing.

Life had settled back to normal over the weeks since my 'accident' and Timothy returning to our lives happy and whole again. It was easy to pretend that things had never been strange or dangerous—we were together now and nothing was going to stand in our way.

I just had to deal with the fact that I was going to be humiliated publicly in front of all my friends and family.

"I still don't know how you found me," I told Timothy, hoping he would drop his guard enough for me to get another taste of his new ice cream flavor.

He shook his head at me teasingly, not fooled in the least. "I've already told you," he said patiently. "I have no idea how I found you. Or how the twins found me. I didn't have any clue who I was in that form, or where I was, or what I was doing. I just felt this drive to be somewhere... and that somewhere was here, at the shop with you."

"Isn't that so romantic?" Iris gushed from where she was painting chocolate rose petals with edible glitter.

It was romantic. It was also a little frustrating. I wanted to know exactly how Timothy had found me. Unfortunately his memory of the whole time was blurry.

"But why did you grab me when I was on fire?" I insisted. "It doesn't make sense at all."

"When I saw you go up in flames," Timothy said seriously, no dimples in sight, "I felt like my world was over. That was when I suddenly remembered who you were and knew I could never, ever, let you go—not matter what."

And he hadn't. Even when holding onto me had almost burned him to death.

"Well I guess I can never doubt your devotion," I teased him, standing on my tiptoes to kiss his lips. "Now, if only you would share your ice cream..."

He playfully pinched my nose. "Nope. Nice try, love. I'm saving this for the party tonight. You should have something to look forward to."

I sighed. I guessed I hadn't succeeded in hiding my lack of enthusiasm about the party from him.

He knew me so well.

It made my insides get all squiggly, realizing that I really had that special relationship with that wonderful man in my life. It was worth everything—every night, every moment of pain, every part of my life that had felt insurmountably difficult—just to have him here.

There was no way I was ever going to let him go again.

Even if I had to fight my father hand-to-hand over it.

The door over the bakery rang, as if triggered by my thoughts.

Sumac bounced into the bakery as if she had never left, as if we were expecting her. She came straight up to the counter and grinned impishly up at me, looking closer to fifteen than the hundred-plus years she claimed was her actual age.

She waggled her fingers at Timothy and my sisters, who all grinned back at her—her energy really was infectious like that. No one could resist her.

Not even me, and I knew that if she was here it probably meant my father had sent her one way or another.

"You won!" Sue crowed, her bright blue eyes twinkling up at me like lit-up sapphires.

I frowned at her, confused. No one was supposed to know the results of the cupcake show, though I'd had several people try to fake me or Iris out just the way Sumac was.

"But," I protested, bending to whisper in her ear. "I didn't win..."

Sumac waved me off with a laugh. "Oh, I'm not talking about that silly thing at all," she chortled. "I'm saying you won. As in, your father has decided that you can keep the Ordinary boyfriend and he won't interfere anymore."

I stared at her with my mouth open. "Are you serious?" I squeaked. "Because, if this is a prank..."

Sumac waved me off again, giggling. "It's not a prank. Even his royal-holiness has to step aside when love is that pure and true." She sighed. "You are so lucky. I was in the cupid business how many years and I never found anything close to this."

I grinned at Timothy. "I really am lucky," I admitted. "Timothy is one in a bazillion."

"And Cindy is one special witch," Timothy said with a wink, swooping down to kiss my cheek.

"Ew," Starrie protested from behind us. "Make them stop, will you? They're way too lovey-dovey. It's making me sick to my stomach!"

I grinned at her, unrepentant. "Just you wait," I warned her. "Someday you're going to feel the same way."

"If you're lucky," Sumac added, her voice wistful. "Ah, well. I'm young yet!" She grinned at us. "So, what does a girl have to do to get a party invite around here?"

"You're welcome to stay," I said immediately. I pointed a finger at her. "Just no cupid Magic, OK? We've already got a baby boom around here, thanks to your last visit."

Sumac grinned. "I make no promises," she said, winking at me significantly.

"No way," I warned her. "I will get revenge. You don't even want to go there."

Her laughter didn't reassure me at all.

Chapter Thirty-Six

The party wasn't really as bad as I thought it was going to be. My whole family as well as some of our most loyal customers all crowded together to watch the show on a big screen TV Timothy had appeared with for the occasion.

I watched, grinning at everyone's reactions when the top came off of my container of cayenne, my head tucked under Timothy's chin. He had one arm draped around my waist, while the other one entwined his fingers with mine.

I had never felt happier or more secure.

The kitten the twins had brought me bounded around the floor after Merlin, trying to pounce on my familiar's fluffy tail. Merlin had an expression of vast patience on his face, but I had a feeling he really liked her.

"Oh, my gosh!" Goldie Locke, my sister exclaimed, as Kane made his non-comment about my cupcakes for the second time. "Can't the guy say a single nice thing about your cupcakes?" She laughed as she caught Kane's eye— he was Iris's date to the party.

He had the good grace to blush. "I couldn't make it too obvious that she was my favorite," he demurred.

"Excuses, excuses," Goldie said, rolling her eyes. She leaned forward, her eyes on the screen. "This is killing me! I need to know who wins like now!"

Timothy's chuckle resonated through me. I smiled up at him. These days I felt like a smile was always plastered to my face. I couldn't help it. I really was ridiculously head-over-heels in love with my boyfriend and it made me just... blissful.

Who cared if my sisters loved to tease me about it nonstop?

Timothy was back! I wanted to sing it out for the world to hear, even if I couldn't carry a tune to save the universe from destruction.

If I sang the universe would probably beg for destruction.

The enormous mountain of snacks Timothy and I had prepared was hugely diminished by the time the results were announced, with much booing and hissing from my loyal audience.

"And you show your face around here," Starrie said, shaking her head at Kane.

"Seriously," Rainey echoed.

"Let's not damage him," Iris said, her voice high with worry.

It looked like it was about to get a little messy, if I knew my family at all. I looked up at Timothy. "How about we get that last batch of gelato served?"

His hand squeezed mine. He followed me to the kitchen, where he swept me up into his arms and planted a kiss on my lips.

The deep fryer hissed a warning that I'd better get my emotions under control.

I giggled and wiggled away from him. "I don't think that was the kind of dessert everyone was expecting," I teased him.

Timothy laughed. "Come on, Cindy. They've seen how we look at each other. Everyone knows we're smooching back here. If we don't we'll just disappoint them all."

"Well, if that's the case," I laughed, shaking my head. I stood on my tip-toes and slid my arms around his neck.

Deep-fryer be damned.

The bell in the front of the bakery rang.

"Cindy!" One of my sisters shouted. "It's somebody for you!"

"Saved by the bell," Timothy muttered behind me as he followed to see who was at the door. "I'm taking that thing down first thing tomorrow."

"Poor bell," I said, shaking my head. "Don't be too cruel to it."

Timothy gave my ponytail a playful tug.

My breath caught as I took in the familiar form waiting near the front door. Her back was to me and I had only seen her once before—briefly—but there was no way I was ever going to forget that face and figure.

Quinna Borden.

Timothy's mother.

My hands tightened on Timothy's.

How was he going to respond, seeing her again—and alive—after all this time? I had been so swept up in having him with me again that I had completely forgotten to mention that I had seen his dead mother—alive and eating—at the bakery.

I turned Timothy to face me. "I think someone is here to see you," I said nervously, feeling my insides quiver. I thought I might actually throw up. "Take as much time as you need. I know this will be... a shock for you."

Timothy looked over my head curiously. I held my breath, waiting for him to stiffen, to exclaim something in shock... anything.

But he didn't.

He just stared across the bakery with a mildly curious expression on his face.

My stomach lurched.

He wasn't surprised then. I guessed that meant he had lied when he told me his mother was dead.

Why would he do something like that? What was he hiding from me?

"I guess you'll want to go talk to her," I said, trying to ignore the pain in my chest that centered somewhere around my heart.

"Why would I want to do that?" Timothy asked in surprise.

"Because," I answered dully, wishing he would just quit with the pretense and admit that he had lied to me about a huge part of his life, "she's your mother."

Timothy laughed incredulously. "My mother's dead," he chided me gently. "I told you that, Cindy. Why would you think that's my mother? I've never seen that woman before in my life."

www.ingramcontent.com/pod-product-compliance
Lightning Source LLC
Chambersburg PA
CBHW051430130726
47987CB00005B/1986